a soft
spot
in the
earth's
skull

I0598576

stories by Jacob Snodgrass

**RED
GIANT
B O O K S**

stories

a soft
s p o t
in the
e a r t h ' s
s k u l l

Cloudy Piss

1

I went to the kitchen for a beer and food, but was stopped in my tracks by the sight of Breeze, wearing nothing but a jockstrap, peeking out the window at the apartment across the way.

"You know our neighbor's a cat serial killer, right?" Breeze went. He'd heard me come into the room, but was too busy to look back. "You hear me, Dave? I guarantee she got a whole crawl space full've dead cats over there. And if you dig up that yard, boy, you gonna find some Stephen King shit down in there."

I made my way past the kitchen table, where Breeze had left a bag of shake, his purple dope pipe and a porno mag with a fat white girl on the cover wearing nothing but some chocolate cake she'd smeared on her tits.

"We're not digging up Becky's yard," I went. "She's harmless. Especially when it comes to cats."

"Depends on what you mean by harmless. If you mean twistin off they tongues and rubbin em all over her privates, then, yeah, she harmless alright."

I could see the conversation was going nowhere fast and let it drop. "Hey, listen," I went, as I opened the fridge, "I'm gonna be getting something to eat here in a sec. That is, if I can find something other than packets of hot sauce and...what are these, melted Lemonheads?...and I'd really appreciate it if your ass crack could find some shelter before then. I'm just funny that way when it comes to food."

Breeze let the blinds clatter shut and looked down at

himself. "Yo, my bad, dude, I forgot I didn't have no pants on."

"Sure, it can happen." I was cradling some withered grapes, some wilted radishes and half a can of peas against my chest. "But why the jockstrap? You don't have any normal underwear?"

Breeze turned away from the window and put his hands on his hips and spread his legs apart, kind of like Superman, if Superman's penis was abundantly on display.

"No, bro, I always wear a jockstrap."

"You always wear a jockstrap?"

"Always, dude." He took his hands from his hips so he could do a swaying motion with one between his legs. "I don't like my stuff swingin all around down there. I know a dude who got his nutsack all twisted up that way once. By time he got to the ER, they thought he was one of them circus freaks that got parts of someone growin out of em. I mean, that's how big one of his nuts had blown up to. He said it was like a cantaloupe, except for it being all red and veiny and shit."

"Sure," I went, and sat down at the kitchen table, watching Breeze's naked ass head into the bathroom where he kept a bag and cardboard box of his belongings.

"Hey, man," Breeze went, as he returned wearing a pair of my sweats he must've fished out of the dirty clothes, "I'm thinkin about startin up a religion. Like, every Sunday we'd get together to worship Krishna and smoke a little weed and listen to Indian music or whatever. And maybe do a little blow."

"That doesn't really sound like a religion."

"Oh, but it is! I mean, I'd be serious about Krishna and shit. I mean, this ain't no joke, because I could totally worship a blue baby. And, you know, I figure if a bunch of us is all focused on him at the same time every week, we're bound to figure some shit out, right?"

"Figure some shit out like what?"

"Like about life, dude," Breeze went, as he tapped some weed from the baggie into his pipe. "Like about the cosmos and angels and shit."

"Angels, huh?" I was only half-listening while I began to plop the radishes and grapes into the can of peas, causing bits of liquid to splash up over the edge. "Man, I'm so hungry. Aren't you hungry? I haven't seen you eat for days."

"That's not true," Breeze went, as he blew smoke from his mouth and offered me the pipe. "Remember that Zagnut? I ate half, and you ate half."

"That was like five days ago."

"Oh."

2

Later that night, I went into the kitchen again, hoping I'd somehow missed something in the fridge, only to find the room thick with weed smoke and Breeze leaning against the counter with a small dog cradled to his chest. "Yo, Dave, you ever see a dog like this? This shit's crazy."

The dog raised its head and pricked up its pointy ears at me.

"Yeah, I've seen those before. It's a Min Pin. So what?"

"I'll tell you so what. This thing's a freak a nature. This isn't no Doberman Pinscher puppy, you know. This an adult." Breeze was sliding his hand under the dog's belly, lifting it up a few inches to show me its size. "Big Girl got this thing three years ago and says it ain't never growed an inch since."

"That's because it's a Min Pin. A Miniature Pinscher. It's not supposed to get any bigger."

"Come on, man, that don't make no sense. Whoever heard of a dog that don't grow?"

"I'm not saying they don't grow. I'm just saying they're supposed to be small. It's the breed."

"Naw man, that mess don't add up. I seen all kinds a Dobermans in my time and ain't none of them stayed this small. So, this either a puppy that ain't growin, which ain't natural, or science figured out a way to make smaller versions of bigger things, which is even more fucked up. I mean, what, scientists got a shrink ray now? But I'll tell you what I think it is. You see that big bag a green over there?"

I glanced toward the bag of weed on the table.

"Yeah, I see it."

"Well, I didn't let her know I seen her, but I seen Big Girl feedin Bo Duke weed outta it. I mean, just sprinklin it on the floor for him to suck up like a Hoover."

Looking from the weed to the dog to Breeze, I went, "And how exactly is that a problem for you?"

"A problem for me?!? You hear what I'm tellin you? It's a problem for Bo Duke, not me. That shit's probably stuntin his growth. I mean, you can't be feedin no dog weed and there not be repercussions. And if she's doin it all the time, which I'm pretty damn sure she is, then his little bones is probably too high to even know they should grow."

"Maybe. But my money's on the shrink ray."

Breeze nodded, but then went, "Wait...the what?"

3

Back then, Breeze was living with me because his girlfriend had kicked him out when she found out about Big Girl being his side chick. It was a crazy time. I was working third shift down at the factory, and it was a shit job with shit hours, and every day I could feel a little more of my life draining away. It was turning me into a zombie. Every morning when my shift ended, I'd leave there with a throbbing headache and aching eyes, and I'd just stare down at my feet as they took me home.

Yet, one day when I had almost reached our apartment, something a bit unusual caught my eye. I'd just rounded the corner to our place when I saw Becky pulling a red wagon bumpily over the grass in front of her place. She was in her thrift store coat that she wore year-round and there was a dingy cloth covering her head. Her face was all red from the heat, and she was skipping, or at least trying to. She'd give it one or two herky-jerky skips, then stumble around, then try it again while the wagon lurched along behind her. And inside the wagon, mixed in with a big lumpy bag of laundry, were two kittens. One orange and one white.

As I got closer, Becky stopped skipping and went back around to the wagon and put one of her fingers in the

kittens' faces and switched it back and forth, until one of
the kittens was finally fed up enough to bat at it. Becky then
burst into a fit of laughter like she'd never seen something
so funny in all her life.

She definitely had a screw loose—there was no doubt
about that—but she wasn't hurting anyone, so what'd I care.
I shrugged, turned away and headed toward our apartment,
but before I even had my keys out, I heard Breeze's voice
come out of nowhere. "She gettin away with cat murder
right under our noses."

"What? Where the hell are you?"

"Yo, shhhhh," Breeze went, and then I saw he was hiding
behind a nearby tree. "Keep your voice down. I'm bout to
break this here case wide open." I looked into his eyes and
saw a crazy glint, and I knew then and there he was coked
out of his mind. Breeze always had theories ("Becky's a
cat killer." "The police are monitoring our apartment with
drones." "The A-rabs at the corner store are poisoning our
milk.") but he only ever acted on them when he'd snorted
up a giant pile of dust.

"Come on, man," I whispered. "Let's get back in the
house before you do something stupid."

"Ain't nothin stupid bout fightin no crime," Breeze
went. And then, before I knew it, he was running out from
behind the tree.

"Oh shit," I went, as Breeze flew past me. I tried to reach
for him; I even got a hold of his shirt for a second, but it
snapped out of my hand as he barreled down our walkway;
and by the time I began to chase after him, he already had a
bead on Becky and was too far ahead for me to do anything

about it.

Like a linebacker, he drove his shoulder into the middle of Becky's back, and I heard a crack like a branch being snapped in half, and her head snapped back and her feet flew out from under her. Breeze left his feet too, and for a moment, the two of them were just floating in the air; and I remember thinking right then that he'd killed her. Surely, he'd broken her back or neck, and probably fucked her up inside too. So, after they fell to the ground, and Becky collided face first with the pavement, it was no surprise at all that she didn't move a muscle. She just laid there perfectly still—I couldn't even tell if she was breathing—and Breeze laid on top of her, panting like a cheetah that had just chased down an antelope.

In all the chaos, the wagon had also been toppled, and as I reached Breeze and Becky, I remembered hearing the kittens meowing, but not seeing them, and thinking they must be trapped under the overturned wagon, but I had to check on Becky before I could worry about them.

I reached down for her, and as I was doing that, Breeze rolled off and into the grass, and she made a sound— something between a gurgle and a whimper—and I remember thinking, "Well, at least she's alive." But then as I grabbed ahold of her sleeve, something else began to dawn on me...something that made my blood run cold, because a few feet away from us, I saw the laundry bag, which had fallen out of the wagon, and saw that something was sticking out of it...and it wasn't dirty clothes. When I leaned in for a better view, I recognized right away what it was: three dead cats hanging out of the bag. And then I realized what made the rest of the bag so lumpy.

My fingers snapped loose from Becky's sleeve, and I looked in horror at Breeze lying on his back in the grass next to her. He was smiling from ear to ear.

"Big ol bag a dead pussies," he went.

4

It only took a week for Breeze to get paranoid enough that he thought he'd better skip town. After the incident with Becky, we placed an anonymous call to the police, and they came out and scooped her up off the ground and carted her off to the hospital and then arrested her, we presumed. Only a couple hours had passed since Breeze had tackled her, and already there was no sign it had ever happened. The wagon was gone, Becky was gone, and the big old bag of dead cats was gone. The coast was clear....clearly clear, in fact...but somehow, after having a week to let it simmer in the murky juices of his mind, Breeze had concluded that the police knew what he'd done to Becky, and that it was just a matter of time before they closed in on him.

"Yo, I gotta get the eff outta Dodge," he went, as me, Breeze and Big Girl sat around the dining room table with Bo Duke sleeping at our feet. "The po po knows I went all *Death Wish* on that crazy bitch."

I shook my head, and Big Girl rolled her eyes.

"Fuck y'all," Breeze went.

He and Big Girl were sitting side by side at the table, and up until then they had been sharing a bomb pop. Breeze would wrap his lips around it and slowly slide it out, and then Big Girl would take it between her lips and do the same, but now Breeze turned his shoulder so she couldn't get her next lick.

"You little shit-ass," she went. She said almost everything with a sneer.

But Breeze ignored her and turned his attention to me instead. "Yo, Dave, listen, let me tell you bout Doc and his so-called wife over in apartment 223." Breeze pointed the bomb pop toward the window and started wagging it at some unknown point in the distance. "Cause that dude's going through the same thing I'm going through, what with being surveilled by the fuzz 24/7, but he been goin through it a lot longer'n me."

"I don't have a clue who you're talking about," I went.

"Yeah you do." Breeze turned his head to the side to lick the bomb pop before it dripped. "He's that one-armed mug that live down there with that real plain-lookin chick. And wait'll I tell you bout what he did with his sickle."

"His sickle?"

"I know, right? That's what I said too. I was like, it ain't enough to be a doctor, but that motherfucker gotta be the grim reaper too?"

"He ain't no doctor," Big Girl went, and she reached forward and snatched the bomb pop clean out of Breeze's hand.

"What?" Breeze went. "Yeah he is too."

"No, he ain't."

"Bitch, please, he tole me so hisself."

"I know. He tells everyone that, but he ain't. He's been

a lotta things. He used to bag groceries at Ms. Allen's place, and he used to be the garbage man for a minute, and he used to be the dog catcher for years, but he ain't never been no doctor. Trust me on that."

Big Girl turned her head from side to side, slurping the bomb pop like her life depended on it, then suddenly bit the tip off and bared her blue-stained teeth at Breeze.

"Jesus, girl," Breeze went. He patted her big thigh and turned his attention back to me. "Listen, whether Doc's a doctor or not ain't important right now…even though he is. What's important is what he did and what come of it. Cause what happen was, about five years ago, Doc and his wife had this dude by the name of Terry McGraw livin with em. I guess Doc and this motherfucker went way back, like they was almost brothers or somethin. So it was all good…except until it wasn't. Cause one day Doc found some photos that Terry had stashed away, and lo and behold if they wasn't nudies of him with Doc's plain jane wife. I mean, you know how it is…sometimes it's the plain ones that's the biggest freaks. But freak or not, you know Doc, and he wasn't gonna stand for no mess like that. So, that night he confronts ol boy, and what you think that motherfucker did?"

"No idea," I went.

"Dude ended up grabbin one of them box cutter-type knives and started slashin the air with it, backin both Doc and his wife into a corner. Now, you know how Doc is, right?"

"No, not really."

"Yeah, you do," Breeze went. "He tries to be real level-headed…real cool…and so he did his best to talk some sense into this Terry dude. Tried to calm his ass down, ya know... but there was nothin that could be done...dude was straight outta his head. So, that's when Doc did what he had to do. It was survival of the fittest up in that bitch, so he snatched up that motherfuckin sickle he kept by the bed and started doin some slicin and dicin of his own."

"Alright, stop," I went, and threw up my hands. "I can't hear another word until I know what's up with this sickle. Give me one good reason why this guy kept a goddamned sickle by his bed."

"Protection, dude," Breeze went. "Why else?"

"I know, but a sickle?"

"I know, man, it's weird as fuck, but who knows, maybe between catchin dogs and the gig with the garbage dudes, Doc was like...I dunno...a grain harvester or somethin." Breeze leaned back toward Big Girl and flopped his head over to look at her. "Hey, Big Girl, that sound bout right to you? You ever hear of ol Doc harvesting or foraging or any shit like that?"

Big Girl rolled her eyes, sneered, and then sucked the remaining bomb pop clean off the stick, which she then threw on the floor for Bo Duke to gnaw on.

"But listen, dude," Breeze went, as he swung his head back around toward me. "All's I know is that he had one, and your boy knew how to use it too, because—and this is exactly how he said it to me—he ripped out Terry's throat with it. You hearin me? Ripped the motherfucker's throat clean out!"

I shook my head. "C'mon...if that's true, then how come he isn't in prison right now? Right this very minute?"

"That's exactly what I'm sayin," Breeze went. "He should be. But for some reason they ain't arrested him yet. But they watchin him. Doc says he sees em all the time... trailin him, watchin him, peepin in his windows. And he says that havin his every move monitored and never knowin when they're finally gonna strike is even worse than bein in prison."

I shook my head. "I don't know, man. That sounds kind of far-fetched."

Breeze fixed me with a stare. "Dude's a doctor, okay? He takes an oath. I don't think he's gonna to be lyin bout something like this. But besides, the point I'm makin is that I can't live like that neither. I gots to be me, I gots to be free, and now I gots to flee. You feel me?"

"No, not really."

"What bout you Big Girl?" Breeze went. "You feel me, don't you?"

Big Girl scrunched up her nose and made a face like she was thinking, but then just shifted over onto her hip and let a slow fart slide out.

"Nice," Breeze went. "I'm out fightin crime, and you's in here destroying the ozone layer with your bean dip ass. Real nice."

And with that, he stood up and made a kissing sound for Bo Duke, who dutifully followed him into the bedroom.

5

The next morning, when I rolled in from work, it seemed like maybe Breeze had chilled on the idea of going on the lam. Lounging deep into the couch and sharing a joint with Big Girl at his side, he wasn't exactly the picture of a man who was about to make a getaway any time soon.

"Dang, girl," Breeze went just as I walked through the door. "He even breathin?" He was using his toes to point at Bo Duke curled up on the floor.

"What you mean, 'Is he breathin?" Big Girl went. "Yeah, he breathin."

"Well, I just figured all that weed might a put him in a coma, that's all."

"Well, he'd still be breathin, dumbass. Ain't like people stop breathin in a coma."

"I dunno....you sure about that? Ain't it like when fish get frozen in the water? Like how they kinda die, but then come back when the water thaws?"

By then, I was already past them and headed into the bedroom, where I was going to flop down face first into the bed. The last thing I remember hearing was Big Girl going, "Damn, Breeze, you the one who needs to start worrying about the weed, not Bo Duke. You seem like you might be turnin retarded."

After that, I was out.

But two hours later, Breeze woke me up. He was practically on top of me, whispering hard into my face.

"Yo, Dave, wake the fuck up! Big Girl just left. We gotta

jet, man. Let's go! Bo Duke needs us!"

I was hardly even awake before we were already on the road. Breeze was at the wheel, and I was riding shotgun, and Bo Duke was on the backseat with his head out the window and little pink tongue flapping in the breeze.

"We good, man," Breeze went, as he switched lanes without using a blinker or even glancing in his mirror. "We got whiskey, we got weed, and we got cocaine. And a couple cans a Vienna sausages for each of us. We good."

"You bring any food for Bo Duke?" I went.

"Oh shit, my bad. He can have some a my sausages."

"Water?"

Breeze just made a face.

6

For a while, we just drove around the outerbelt, circling the city several times, because Breeze was too high to find the exit he wanted. But I didn't really care. It was a sunny day, hot as hell, but we had the windows down and were speeding along, and I was sipping from the whiskey and dozing off here and there. Breeze brought some CDs with him—some spaced-out stuff and some rappers I'd never heard of—but it was one of those days where everything sounded good. And eventually Breeze found that magic exit he'd been seeking and took it, and then drove for miles and miles, past towns we knew at first, and then past ones we didn't later on, until I was pretty sure we were lost. But it didn't matter—I was just along for the ride, knowing Breeze would eventually wear down, and then I'd motor us back home from wherever we were. It was all good. Even the Vienna sausages.

7

By the time we stopped for gas and to change drivers, I had no idea where we were. Between the whiskey and the weed, I was pretty tore up when I slid behind the wheel— we both were—and I just started driving toward some big water tower I saw off in the distance. It seemed as good a direction to go as any.

Breeze must've been even more tore up than me, though, because he was seriously slurring, and we weren't even a mile down the road before his talk turned kind of serious.

"I gotta get me some balance, bro," Breeze went. "I mean it. I was bein for real the other day when I was talkin about those angels and that blue-ass baby and shit."

"Yeah? You think those'll give you some balance?"

"Naw, not them alone, but they'll help, ya know. Kinda show me the way. I mean, I'm just sayin, it's like how I gotta save Bo Duke here before he gets put in a coma he ain't never comin out of, and how I gotta save all those cats from crazy bitches like Becky, and how I gotta just keep doin shit like that to balance it all out, man. You know, balance out all the bad shit I've done, and all the bad shit I just keep on doin."

For a few minutes after that, neither of us said anything. I wanted to say something—I wanted to make him feel better—but I just couldn't think of what to say. So, I just kept quiet and stared out the window and concentrated on the water tower and the blazing sun behind it like they were the only things in the world that really mattered.

Eventually, Breeze broke the silence. "You know it wasn't just Big Girl that got my ass kicked to the curb?"

"No?"

"No. She found out about the marriages too."

"All of them?"

"Yep. All three."

I knew what the deal was with the marriages. I knew they were just for money, but I could also see how that might not sit so well with a girlfriend. Breeze had married all three girls—and in fact was still married to all three— because they needed US citizenship, and in exchange they each gave him five thousand dollars cash. It was a pretty good little scam he had going...but yeah, it'd take a pretty special girlfriend to be okay with it, I guess.

"And them pills sure as hell didn't help none neither," Breeze went.

"Pills?"

"Yeah, man, they showed up in the mail when I wasn't there, so she opened em. A giant bottle of penis enlargement pills. I mean, a giant fucking bottle. And then about a minute later the phone started to ring."

"Big Girl?" I went.

"Yep."

"Running her mouth?"

"Yep." Breeze pointed me toward a gas station in the distance where we could get some beer since we'd killed the whiskey long before. "I was doomed every which way but loose."

8

I was hoping the beer would cheer Breeze up, but it turned out there was something inside that gas station that cheered him up even more than beer. There was a little pizza joint attached to the gas station, and while we were at the counter waiting to pay for our beer, we heard some jukebox music. It was country music—the shitty new kind, not the good old kind—so we hardly even noticed it at first. But then, as the lyrics kicked in, we heard every single voice in the pizza joint start singing along, and that's when we took notice. I mean, it sounded like there were a hundred people in there all singing their hearts out. It was crazy.

"Yo, man," Breeze said to the cashier, "let me leave this beer here for a second, chief. I gotta see this shit for my own two eyes."

In order to get into the pizza joint, we had to go around a corner. So, it wasn't until we were in the joint itself that we saw that all of that singing was coming from about thirty people, not a hundred, but man were they belting it out and having a good time.

The place was crazy, and it sure didn't look like your average pizza joint. The lights were all down real low like it was a nightclub, and there were some flashing colored lights over near the bar that turned everything blue and red. There were a few people sitting down at the tables and eating pizza, but most were up and dancing or over at the bar, and every single one of them was singing at the top of their lungs.

"This shit's off the chain!" Breeze shouted to me over the noise.

I was glad to see that he had a huge smile on his face. We headed over to the bar and ordered a couple beers and shots, and then found a booth where we could soak it all in.

"Check out your girl over there," Breeze went, as he pointed toward a woman dancing around over by the bar. She was short and fat and was wearing an orange leather coat and a sequined cowboy hat. It took me a second to notice that she was also barefoot, and that her ankles were all purple and swollen like logs of baloney.

I looked back at Breeze and raised my eyebrows, but he was already looking at something else. Dancing out in the middle of the room were three women who looked almost identical to one another—all skinny, all white, all bleached blonde—who were carrying around a full-sized, unfurled American flag. Around them, a circle of guys— some wearing cowboy hats and some wearing ball caps— were dancing and grinding up against the girls. One of them had on a t-shirt that said: I'M NOT ALWAYS A DICK- -JUST KIDDING, GO FUCK YOURSELF; but most of them just had on flannel shirts, or black t-shirts, or no shirt at all. And there were some fat girls out there too, shaking their money makers and wearing cut-off jean shorts and halter tops that seemed to be holding on for dear life. The drinks were flowing fast and free, and everyone was a-hootin' and a-hollarin' and a-sweatin' and a-laughin'. Faces were flushed and eyes were glassy, and it seemed like there was always someone raising their arms up in praise of something: America, Jesus, The South, booze, or pussy.

Breeze couldn't get enough of it. The unbridled energy of the scene just tripped him out. Of course, it didn't hurt that we were both pretty smashed, too, and getting more and more smashed by the minute, because as soon as we'd finish one drink, Breeze was off getting us more, until he finally drank so much that he eventually forgot what he was doing and instead of getting us drinks, ended up out there dancing and grinding and shouting out, "Yippee ki-yay, motherfuckers!"

I'd never known Breeze to listen to a single note of country music in his life, but he instantly fit right in, and before I knew it, he was making friends with everyone and passing around a J; and a little later, he was off in a corner, tongue kissing with one of those skinny blondes.

In fact, that's where I found him when it was time to go. The lights had been clicked on, and the waitresses were sweeping up the floor and bussing the tables for one last time. When I reached Breeze, he and the blonde were still in each other's arms as they were saying their goodbyes, and Breeze had one hand down the back of her shorts. As they parted, the blonde told Breeze her phone number, and he pointed at his head and went, "I got it, girl," but I knew there wasn't a chance.

Breeze and I then started to make our way out of the place, but before we got to the door, the cashier from the gas station side came trotting up to us with our case of beer in his hand.

"Wait!" he said. "You guys still buying this or you want me to put it back?"

"That was hours ago, my man," Breeze went. "That shit's gotta be warm as piss."

"Yeah, but still…" the cashier said, and Breeze looked at the guy like he was crazy and started to shake his head, but then he stopped and a weird look crossed his face.

When I saw that, a weird one must've crossed mine too, because we'd both realized the same thing at the same time. We'd been in that pizza joint for hours, just screwing around and getting drunk and wasting time, and all that time we'd forgotten poor Bo Duke out there in the car in that stifling heat with the windows rolled all the way up.

"Fuck, fuck, fuck, fuck…" Breeze went.

We both bolted toward the door, and then as soon as we pushed through it, we started running toward the car. But even as we ran, I knew we were just going through the motions. There was nothing we could do…not a thing. You heard about these sorts of things on the news all the time, and they never ended well. You'd hear about a baby that had been left in a hot car, and you'd picture its beet red face as it screamed and cried, until the heat became so suffocating that its cries were smothered in its throat. And I knew that was what we were racing toward. I knew it before we even reached the car. Poor Bo Duke didn't stand a chance.

Breeze got there just before I did. "Fuck, fuck, fuck, fuck, fuck…"

"Can you see him?" I went, as I came skidding to a stop.

"No! Fuck! Look at this shit!" Breeze went, as he jerked open the driver's side door. All around us—everywhere under our feet—there was shattered glass.

"They fuckin took him!" Breeze went, as he dove into the car and started frantically searching for Bo Duke. "The fuckers busted out the window and took him!"

Through the broken window, I watched Breeze crawl over the front seat and into the back, which was littered with hundreds of small squares of glass. "They fuckin' took him!" Breeze squeezed himself down onto the floor and began to desperately feel around under the seats, hoping he'd somehow find Bo Duke cowering down there.

It was hopeless. He was definitely gone.

I turned away from the car and looked up and down the road, wondering which way he'd gone. It was well past midnight, pitch black, and still hot enough that little prickles of sweat had begun to bead up on the back of my neck. Slowly, I let my eyes close. I felt exhausted all the way to the bone.

"Dave!" I heard Breeze going. "Ain't you gonna help me, man? Dave!"

I kept quiet. I didn't move an inch.

9

Breeze and I slept for three hours, and then it took us eighteen to get back home, but we made it.

"Check this shit out," Breeze went, as he eased the car into our parking lot. "They probably talkin bout us."

Big Girl, Doc and his plain-looking wife were out in front of our apartment, talking a million miles an hour.

"Maybe," I went, "but I bet it's about that instead." I pointed toward Becky, who was sitting out on her stoop.

For a second, Breeze looked pissed, but then he just shook his head and went, "Ain't that some shit," as he pulled into a parking spot.

We sat there for a few seconds looking at her. She had on a house arrest ankle bracelet. There were no cats anywhere to be seen. She looked about as glum as you can get.

"She stupid, you know that?" Breeze went.

"I can't argue with you there," I went.

"Look at her. She look like a fat toad squattin down on a mushroom top."

"Yeah, something like that."

"And she ain't even tryin, you know that?"

"Trying to look like a toad?"

"Naw man," Breeze went. "I mean tryin to strike any sorta balance in her life. I mean, I might not be gettin it right all the time, but at least I'm tryin. But this toad here, she ain't even tryin...she just bad all the time. I mean, 24/7, seven days a week, like she the Waffle House of bad."

By then, Big Girl had broken up her little powwow with Doc and his wife, and was headed over to us.

"Where you two shitbirds been?" she went, as she leaned down to look in at Breeze.

"Fantasy Island, baby," Breeze went. "Tattoo done hooked us up with some a his midget bitches. Two for the price a one."

Big Girl just sneered.

"Look, Big Girl," Breeze went, "I gotta tell you something bout Bo Duke."

"What? I been lookin for his little shit-ass all morning."

"Well, you ain't gonna find him."

"I ain't? How the hell you so sure about that?"

Breeze took a deep breath. "Cause I saved him."

"What you mean, 'Saved him'?!?"

"You know, like Jesus of Nazz, I saved him from this here world of sin."

"Oh, so you Jesus now, huh?" Big Girl went.

"Just in my spare time." Breeze started up the car and began to slowly back out.

"Where the fuck you going now?!?" Big Girl went.

"Titty bar," Breeze went, and started to roll up his window. "It's the way Bo Duke would have wanted it, don't you think?"

The Story About the Funeral

It felt as if all of the sun's heat was solely focused on their backs, as Jack and Douglas made their way down Broad Street, feeling beads of sweat blossoming on their necks before bursting and trickling down into the collars of their shirts. Since leaving the last bar, they hadn't walked far, but already were watching for another one to duck into, so long as it offered cold beer and AC. Far ahead, where everything was touched by a sort of rippling illusion brought on by the heat, they could see the stretch of buildings that lined both sides of the street start to rise with the incline of the road. After that, however, everything began to swiftly dip down and disappear at the river's edge, which was hidden from Jack and Douglas, but was hinted at by a sort of blinding clarity that the water lent to the sky above it. In less oppressive heat, they surely would have walked as far as the water before stopping again, and likely even would have crossed over the bridge and meandered through the neighborhoods on the other side, but instead they only ventured a few more blocks before Jack gestured toward a quaint-looking bar on the other side of the street, and Douglas eagerly nodded his agreement.

At a trot, they crossed the street and went into the bar, which seemed, at first, to be as dark as a closet, so marked was the difference between it and the sun-drenched world they'd just left behind. Seated at the bar itself, a few men— mere silhouettes to Jack and Douglas's constricted eyes— silently sipped their beers, and the only sound in the whole place came from an AC unit that rattled and hissed in the window. Jack ordered a couple beers before they eased their way toward a booth at the back of the room where they could talk without disturbing the others.

"At the last place," Douglas said after taking his first drink, "you were about to tell me something about your uncle, but that guy in that crazy trapper hat interrupted you."

"Yeah. I wanted to tell you about his funeral."

Jack took a sip of his beer and smiled at how cold it was. Then he looked across the table at Douglas—a man he had been friends with for nearly twenty years—and parted his lips to tell him about this uncle, but before he could utter a single word, the man in the trapper hat—the very same man who had interrupted their conversation at the last bar—walked through the front door.

"Look who it is," Jack said with a nod, and Douglas turned to see.

"And he's not alone," Douglas said, as the two friends watched the silhouettes of the man in the hat and a woman at his side gradually become fleshed out as they strolled toward them. The man was tall, but with a large belly, and terribly scraggly hair. Yet, the woman was quite pretty and had lively, smiling eyes.

The man reached their booth, took off his hat and used one of his hands to pull back his tangled hair from his forehead. "See those scars?" he said, repeating what he said to them at the last bar when he had also approached them and pulled his hair back from his forehead. Yet, there were no scars to see. The man was merely wrinkling up his forehead, trying hard to create the illusion of scars.

However, to be polite, just as he had done at the last bar, Jack said, "Sure, I see them."

"I got those wrasslin' down in Mexico," the man said.

"Pro wrasslin', ya know. I wrassled all the greats. Abdullah the Butcher, Mil Mascaras, Bruiser Brody, all a them. Brody was the worst, though. He'd beat you with a chair, gouge out your eyes, split ya wide open. It was him that done most a these scars. But outside a the ring, he was the nicest man ya could meet. A real pussycat. He'd buy ya a steak, buy ya a drink, give ya the shirt off his back. Just an all-around good guy."

Having shown off his faux mementos, the man let his hair tumble back down over his face, and then stood there looking at Jack and Douglas, like a dog awaiting praise.

Jack shot a glance at Douglas, and then looked back at the man. "That's really something," Jack said, "but, if you don't mind, my friend and I here are trying to have a conv—"

"You wanna arm wrassle?" the man interrupted.

For a second, Jack went silent, staring at the man while this unexpected question hung in the air between them.

"What? No, I don't want to arm wrestle."

"Why? Ya scared?" The man winked at the woman at his side, who started nodding her head and widening her smile.

"No, I'm not scared. I just don't want to. Like I said, we're trying to have a conversation here, and—"

"I'll do it," Douglas said. "I'll arm wrestle you."

"What? Why?" Jack said, as he looked into his friend's eyes, trying to gauge in that split second whether the drinks they'd been sharing that afternoon had caught up with him, but Douglas just smiled and shrugged. "Alright, Douglas, do whatever you want. What do I care? No one's stopping you."

Jack rolled his eyes and slumped back into his seat, determined to have nothing to do with it. Yet, even at that moment, as his contempt for such foolishness was beginning to roil inside him, he couldn't fend off a fleeting pang of regret that seized hold of him as he caught a glimpse of the woman and saw how her eyes lit up when she looked at the two other men.

"Well, hotdog!" The man in the hat rubbed his hands together before hastily rolling up his sleeve and plunking his elbow down on the table.

Douglas took a more reserved approach, leaning forward and limply propping his arm up on the table. He then gave the man a wide smile, as if he was about to pull off some outrageous prank, rather than have his arm yanked clean out of the socket. The man didn't even notice the smile. He was too charged up to notice much of anything. His shoulders were hunched and taut, and his breathing had become a ragged combination of hisses and snorts.

Without a word from either man—as if they were responding to some silent, internal signal—they simultaneously leaned toward one another and their hands met. Their forearms stiffened, and the tendons beneath their skin grew taut.

The woman also leaned in toward them; she, too, was reacting to a soundless signal deep within herself. Jack, however, resolutely remained back in his seat. He did not turn his eyes away; to have done so would have given too much credence to their callow act; but as he watched them, his expression remained unwaveringly blank.

The woman, whose smiling face was levitating only a few inches away from their coiled fists, said, "1-2-3...Go!" and the two men lurched into action. Their hands, strangling one another, trembled with tension as they immediately settled into a stalemate, but then, like a tree falling in slow motion, their arms began to steadily tilt one way, and to the surprise of everyone, that way was in the favor of Douglas.

"Come on!" the woman urged. "Fight!"

And her man did fight...even after the inevitable outcome had become clear. With eyes bulging and spittle forming on his lower lip, he tried with all his might to stave off defeat, but before the woman's words were even done ringing in his ears, the thud of the two men's arms collapsing onto the table drowned it out.

"Woohoo!" Douglas hooted and thrust his hands up in victory, but his celebration was short-lived, for when he saw the man hang his head and tightly cross his arms over the dome of his belly, Douglas lowered his arms and quickly tapered off his whooping into nervous laughter. Yet, the damage had been done. Before Douglas had even checked himself, the woman had sidled up to him and wrapped her hands around one of his arms, caressing his bicep.

"Oooo," she purred. "Now, this is a real man."

"Now, you cut that out!" the man with the hat said.

"Why, jealous? Jealous of a *real man*?"

The man's face turned crimson, and he started to sputter, but no words actually came out. Instead, he forsook words for action, grabbing the woman by the arm and yanking her away. And although she quickly snatched her arm back from him, and gave one last admiring glance back at Douglas, she still followed him as he headed off into the shadows, and then out the front door and back into the merciless sunlight.

"Well, you must be proud," Jack said as soon as the door closed behind the couple.

"Not really," Douglas said. "It was just for a laugh."

"It didn't seem like a laugh to him."

"No. But he'll get over it." Douglas held up his empty beer bottle. "Want another?"

Jack looked at his own empty bottle. There was part of him that would have liked to have left the bar, and left behind the childishness that his friend had just engaged in, but he knew his feelings would pass, and he didn't relish the thought of going back out into that harsh sunlight just yet, so he said, "Sure, why not. One more."

Jack watched his friend walk over to the dimly lit bar where he became another silhouette, like the men who were already seated there; and after Douglas ordered their beers, Jack could hear his muffled voice and laughter as he chatted with one of the patrons. Douglas was like that; he made friends easily; he was comfortable in his own skin, no matter the setting. Jack had always known they were different in that way, but that was nothing new, and he mostly appreciated the difference. It was only every so often that he found it vaguely distasteful.

"Here you go," Douglas said when he returned and handed Jack his beer. Jack thanked him, and then they both fell silent for a moment—each sipping his beer and savoring the stinging coldness of it—before Douglas broke the silence by saying, "Now, tell me this story about your uncle that keeps getting interrupted."

"I'm almost afraid to start. It might summon him back."

The two men chuckled.

"But you must be brave." Douglas raised his bottle as if to toast to his friend's courage.

"I'll do my best." Jack raised his bottle and clinked it against his friend's, and the two men chuckled again.

"I may have mentioned this uncle to you once or twice before." Jack settled back into his chair. "I don't know. He's my uncle Craig, my mom's brother. We used to see him all the time when I was a kid. He'd be at all the family gatherings, and he even worked with my dad for a while at the lithographing plant, so he was always around. And back then, I thought he was great. He was the kind of uncle who'd take the time to talk with the kids, and he was funny, and he liked things that we could relate to, like horror films and science fiction, so we all thought he was great. And he was...he really was. But then as I got older, I started to see less and less of him. You know how it is? You go off to college, get a job and all that, and you just lose touch for a while. So, he started to kind of fade out of my life. But then, at some point—maybe right after college or right around then—I was back home hanging out at a family get-together with my mom and a few other relatives, and my uncle Craig was there, and it was one of those moments where you start to see someone for the first time as they really are. You know what I mean? It was one of those times where, for the first time as an adult, I was starting to see what all the other adults had been like all along. But don't get me wrong, my uncle wasn't a bad guy. He was just...how do I put this...well, he just got on people's nerves, I guess. I mean, he was just really needy. He just talked and talked and talked, and he didn't know when to quit, you know. He just needed everyone's attention, no matter what. And that was something about him I'd just never noticed before."

"I think I know the type," Douglas said. "Was he really jokey? Usually that type's really jokey."

"Yes, exactly! Everything was either a joke with him, or...I don't know...very staged...very rehearsed. But don't get me wrong—he could actually be funny. I mean, sometimes he was, but it was very much a quantity over quality type of humor, so that it just wore you down. After a while, you weren't even laughing, even if it was funny. But that didn't stop him. If anything, it made him try even harder."

"Oh yeah," Douglas interrupted, "I've definitely suffered through a few conversations like that in my time."

"Right, right...we all have. But back then, I was still young—just out of college or whatever—and you just didn't notice stuff like that when you were younger. But that night, I remember really noticing it, and it just seemed so...I don't want to say pathetic, because that seems so harsh... but, I don't know...it seemed sad...just sad. I mean, I just remember sitting there listening to him for what seemed like forever, and then suddenly I just couldn't listen any more. I couldn't take it. I got up like I was going to the restroom or something, and I just never came back. Just disappeared into a room where no one else was and read for the rest of the night, until my parents found me and said they were going home."

"Ah, yes," Douglas said, "the old quick escape."

"Exactly," Jack said. "But here's the thing. Over the years, I came to see that the way he acted that night was just the tip of the iceberg, because he was so needy...such a narcissist, I guess you'd say...that he'd get attention anyway he could, even if that meant making up lies. And I don't just mean lies to make himself look good. In fact, just the opposite. The lies often made him look bad, or even made our family look bad. Whatever got him attention, it didn't matter. Like, at some point...he must've been in his forties by then...he started going to AA. He started telling everyone, kind of out of the blue, that he was an alcoholic, and he started going around trying to make amends and all that. You know, doing all of the steps and going to meetings all the time. But there was just one problem."

"What's that?" Douglas said.

"He wasn't an alcoholic."

"What?"

"I know, I know...but it's the truth. I mean, sure, he drank, but he drank like we all drink, not like an alcoholic drinks. And if you need any proof that he wasn't really an alcoholic, then all you need to know is that when he tried to quit, he did it without any problems. Like it was nothing. No relapses, no struggles, no mood swings, nothing. Cold turkey, and that was that. If anything, he was happier than ever. And I don't mean after he finally got clean, but right away...a week after he started up with the meetings. And you know why?"

"Because he wasn't an alcoholic in the first place?" Douglas said.

"Well, partly. But also because the whole stunt not only got him attention from family and friends, but he now had a captive audience at those meetings."

"Oh no, that's true," Douglas said. "Those poor souls. They're already suffering, and then they had to listen to him."

"Oh yes, exactly. But here's the kicker."

"Wait—there's more?"

"Much. But I'm not going into it all...I'm just giving you one example. So, here's the kicker, okay? Once he wasn't getting as much attention from his alcoholism racket, he started up a new one. He started saying he'd been molested. And get this, he said it was his mom who did it."

"His mom?"

"Yes, his mom. My grandmother. And there's no truth to it at all! Not a shred! My mom, who lived in the same house that they did—who grew up right alongside my uncle—says he's completely full of shit. And all of her brothers, and anyone who has ever known my grandmother says the same thing—he's completely full of shit. But he couldn't stop himself. He couldn't resist it. No matter how bad it made him look, and no matter how bad it made my grandmother look, and no matter how it broke her heart, and what it did to my family, he couldn't quit. He couldn't resist. He just had to have the attention, no matter how he got it...no matter who he hurt doing it."

"My god, what a piece of work." Douglas shook his head and a smile of disbelief spread across his face.

"You said it." Jack took a big swallow of his beer, then nodded the bottle toward Douglas. "And that brings me up to the funeral, which I had to go all the way back home for last week. And like every funeral for everyone I ever grew up with—every single person in my entire hometown—it was at this little old funeral home called Embrey's, where everyone back there has their funeral. And as I expected, everyone was there—the whole family, all his friends, and even people from around town that I didn't even know really knew him—but that's how all of the funerals back there are. But it was a good turnout, and I was glad to see it. He might've been a piece of work, but in the end, you still hope he goes out right, you know."

"That's true," Douglas said. "Everyone deserves at least that."

"Yeah," Jack said. "So, it all went well...it was nice...and then we all went to the Presbyterian church in town where my whole family goes, and we had lunch in the basement that the old ladies from the church made for us. The same lunch they always prepare...rigatoni in some red sauce, a little salad in a styrofoam bowl, and some weak iced tea. And then when I was done with that, and had gotten up and was ready to go back to my parents' house, one of the guys from the funeral that I didn't even really know was friends with my uncle—this guy named Mitch Talson—came up to me and started telling me about how he knew my uncle through AA."

"He just completely outed him, huh?" Douglas said.

"Yeah, he must've missed out on the anonymous part," Jack said with a little laugh, "because he just launched right into my uncle's business. Of course, what did it matter? My uncle had been telling the whole town his business for years, and besides, we'd just buried him...what does he care now, right? But here's the part that killed me...here's what made the whole thing so crazy. Mitch is going on and on about AA...kind of halfway telling me about my uncle, but also kind of telling me his own story at the same time...and I'm only halfway listening, but then all of a sudden I hear him go, 'Since you know how much your uncle suffered, you can imagine what it was like for me, not only being cross-addicted to alcohol and cocaine, but to have been molested by *both* of my parents.' And that's when it hit me... this guy is actually trying to one-up my uncle in the misery department at my uncle's own funeral!"

"Wow," Douglas said, "that takes some nerve."

"Right," Jack said. "That's what you'd think, but it's not even nerve...it's something else. More like a compulsion."

"Just like your uncle."

"Exactly!"

"But even worse!"

"Right!" Jack said. "But let me tell you this last part. Let me tell you what I said to him. After he'd gone on and on... and believe me, he went on and on forever...telling me all about the molestation, and how he didn't have shoes growing up, and how he had to kill a chicken just so he'd have something to eat, and how all his addictions were his parents' fault, not his. After all that, he then started to tell me about his recovery, and the whole time he's telling me, he's taking little jabs at my uncle, like to point out how much better his recovery was than his."

"Trying to one-up him again," Douglas said.

"Yes, exactly...even trying to one-up him on recovery. And so finally, I'd heard enough. I just needed to get away from this guy and be on my way. But before I finally escaped, I had to leave him with something to chew on. A little nugget to stick in his craw, you know. So, right before I go...and I know this is an asshole move, but I couldn't help it...I said to him, 'I don't know if you know it or not, Mitch, but about an hour before the funeral, we found out that the mortician molested my uncle while he was embalming him. Can you believe it? Even in death, my uncle had to suffer.'"

"No, you didn't!" Douglas said.

"I did!"

"And what'd he say?"

"Well, I don't know if he was dumbfounded or angry or what, but he didn't say anything. He just stood there staring at me with his mouth hanging open. And so I just said, 'So, top that,' and walked away."

"Oh man, Jack, you're my hero."

Jack threw his head back and laughed, and said, "I don't know if I should have said it or not...I mean, I'm not exactly proud of it...but it was just one of those things. I just couldn't resist."

"No, no," Douglas said, "he had it coming. You were well within your rights."

"Maybe," Jack said with a little laugh. "But, still."

Douglas smiled and nodded at him. Then he took the last swallow of his beer. "One more?" he said, showing Jack the empty bottle.

"Sure, why not," Jack said, smiling. "One more, and then we'll hit the road."

Jack watched his friend make his way back over to the bar, and after ordering their beers, he could hear Douglas talking and laughing with the other patrons, just has he had done before, and Jack felt himself smiling along with them, even though he couldn't make out what they were saying. Whatever it was, he knew it would be clever, because Douglas was always quick with a clever comment. Jack admired that about him, maybe even envied him for it. But it was just one of those small differences that they had between them. Jack was good at some things that Douglas wasn't, and Douglas was good at some things that Jack wasn't. It's just how it was, and Jack figured it was part of what made them such good friends.

When Douglas got back, he laughed a little as he handed Jack his beer.

"What?" Jack said, laughing a little too.

"Oh, nothing. I just had a funny thought, that's all."

"What?"

"Oh, it was stupid. But, you know, as I was walking over here, it just occurred to me...it just kind of crossed my mind...what if they weren't lying? I mean, how do you know for sure?"

"Who?" Jack looked confused.

"Your uncle, and what's-his-name?"

"*Mitch?*"

"Yeah, Mitch, right! I just started thinking about them, and I mean, that's just your perception of them. You think they're lying, and they sure sound like they're lying, *but how can you be sure?*"

"What?" Jack said, and the look of confusion on his face deepened. "It's not just my perception; it's everyone's. I mean, there's no evidence...none! But there's an awful lot of evidence that those guys are out-and-out liars. Always have been and always will be."

"Right, right." Douglas took a quick sip of his beer. "All I'm saying is that you can never be entirely sure of anything, right? I mean, one hundred percent sure."

"What?" Jack shook his head and gave his friend a look of bewilderment. "Of course you can."

"But no, I mean...well, take the example of how we've all heard of legal cases where all of the evidence seems to clearly point toward a certain person, and everyone is completely convinced that they're guilty, right? I mean, before there's even a trial, we've already publicly convicted them. But then, presto! Some unforeseen piece of evidence crops up, and it changes *everything*. What everyone thought was a sure thing is now turned completely on its head."

"Okay, sure, whatever," Jack said. "You can never be *one hundred percent* sure about anything...I'll give you that... but you can be pretty damn close! And, trust me, with these guys, that's how it is. They're liars! Everyone knows it...it's crazy to even question it!"

"Okay, but forget them," Douglas said, shaking his head. "I'm not talking specifically about them anymore. I'm talking generally. I'm talking about how people...not just your uncle and Mitch, but anyone...how people don't even really know themselves, let alone know someone else."

Jack started to say something, but stopped and stared at his friend for a moment, trying to gauge the situation—trying to determine how serious *and how sober* his friend was.

"What in the hell are you talking about?"

"Don't get all bent out of shape," Douglas said. "All I'm saying is that who we are in our heads is a lot different than who we present ourselves to be, and if you factor in that our own minds hide things from us, then you start to wonder if we even have a chance of ever knowing who we really are."

Douglas paused and gave Jack a long look to see if he knew what he meant, but Jack's face was blank, and all he did was silently lean back into his seat. Douglas tried to clarify. "I mean, when you think about it, you can even make an argument that those guys who lie all the time are as truthful as any of us, because what we're showing the world is just as much of a lie. Hell, it might even be more of a lie. You know what I mean?"

"No. No, I don't."

Douglas opened his mouth to spell out his point, but saw by his friend's expression that further clarification wasn't welcomed. He leaned into his seat, and for a few moments, the two men sat in silence, drinking their beers, neither of them satisfied with the direction their conversation had taken.

After a bit, though, it seemed to Douglas that it was his place to break the silence—his place to say a simple word or two (because he knew that was all it would take) to break the pall of discontent that hung over them...but every time a word came to his lips, he suppressed it, causing the silence between him and his friend to grow even more difficult to breach. It wasn't until both had finished their beers that one of them spoke. It was Jack, not Douglas, who said, "I think it's time."

Douglas nodded. The men placed their empty bottles on the table, but neither stood up. Everything around them was shadow, and they knew that everything outside was unforgiving light.

Couch, Then Coffin

1

"Oh yeah, right, the Fourth of July."

That was Harry's first thought when he woke up in complete darkness. It was the muffled sound of *bang-bang-bang* that had awakened him.

His next thought was of his fiancee, Bethany; his hand resting on her knee; their heads lolling together as they watched the fireworks on TV.

Then, after that, he thought: "Couch, then coffin?"

But he wasn't quite ready for that thought, so he permitted it to be nudged aside by one more: Bethany's dad, Warren, bending over to pick up a sparkler he'd dropped in the grass.

Warren was twice Harry's age, but was in top physical condition. Whereas Harry, who'd even been a little lumpy back in his Navy days, had gone all soft. It made Harry uncomfortable to watch Warren's form-fitting cargo shorts, illuminated by the moonlight, tightening around his muscular legs, while Harry, with his belly hanging over his waistband, sat off to the side holding Bethany's hand.

Perhaps the next logical thought might've been: "You need to get your life in order, Harry! You've got to diet and join a gym and get yourself fit!"

But it was too late to mull over such lifestyle changes. The more pressing matter at hand had to be acknowledged.

So, dutifully, Harry tried to sit up, but his forehead collided with a surface that was only inches above him. When his hands and arms got into the act and began to frantically, almost involuntarily, flail about, they found themselves quite restricted by the narrow confines around him.

It was then that all of Harry's other thoughts went whoosh, like dead leaves gathered up in a great wind, and all that was left behind in his mind was one thought...*one single, sickening word*: COFFIN.

That's all it took. Harry started screaming his head off, and for a while there, you'd have thought he was never going to shut up.

****

The funny thing about screaming your head off, though, is that you can only do it for so long. Eventually, you'll go hoarse, and once you're hoarse, that's it, you're hoarse... you're useless. And besides that, even in a white-hot panic of slimy-wet blubbering, you eventually realize how futile your efforts are, and so you pull yourself together, maybe even in mid-scream, the way Harry did. Bam! He cut that caterwauling off like a faucet and started going *Gotta think, Gotta think, Gotta think* instead.

Now, that was more like it. More like what you'd expect from a man who'd not only been the back-up quarterback for his junior high football team, but who'd also spent six years in the Navy. And while it's true that he'd been dishonorably discharged halfway through his second term, that doesn't mean the whole six years was for naught. As Harry was fond of pointing out, he learned any number of skills as a Seaman—everything from firefighting to hand-to-hand combat—but most importantly, he'd learned a discipline of the mind. That, more than anything, was what was going to get him out of that damned box and up through the six feet of densely packed earth that separated him from freedom.

So, Harry set himself to thinking in earnest. He thought first about whether he'd ever encountered such a situation before, and as you might expect, it didn't take long for him to answer with a resounding "No." But then he thought about whether he'd ever heard of anyone being in such a situation before, and to his surprise, two people quickly came to mind.

The first was Harry Houdini, whose story he'd been attracted to as a child because of their shared given name; and the second was Batman—particularly an issue of *Detective Comics*, also encountered in childhood, in which the dark knight found himself buried alive.

Both seemed like potentially promising leads, and so starting with the former, Harry thought, "Okay, what do I remember about Houdini? Come on, think! Think! He was muscular, right? Right! And he had wavy hair. Or was it was just curly? Oh, who the heck cares, Harry...how does his hair help at a time like this?! Think! Think! What else do you know? Come on! You were endlessly getting those books out of that darn library...What else was in them? Oh, I know! I know!... He was always chained up, wasn't he? Heavy chains...Yes! Yes!...And he was muscular and chained up and always had his shirt off. Yes, yes, that's it! Okay, then...So how'd he get out? How'd he manage to slip those chains off his body?"

Harry's thoughts, which had been quite frantic to that point, screeched to a halt, and he said out loud, "Oh Ho!" as he realized that he had become aroused to the point of erection.

Now, to say this was a pleasant surprise would probably be an overstatement given the circumstances, but it was a surprise nonetheless, because Harry had been experiencing, shall we say, a pronounced lack of turgidity in his life for the past several months. In fact, his whole libido had been a no show for some time, which had naturally caused a tension to grow between him and Bethany.

Yet, there he was, languishing under six feet of earth, when he surprisingly stiffened. It was a promising development—even buried Harry recognized that—but one which he had no time to dwell on at that moment.

"Come on, you silly bugger," Harry said. "Go down! Go down! There's only so much room in here for the two of us!"

Fortunately, that stern talking to seemed to do the trick, as Harry's member began to melt, and he did his best to move his mind away from Houdini and over to Batman.

"Okay, what do I remember about Batman?" Harry thought. "Come on, think! Think!" And although it'd been years since he'd read *any* comic book, let alone the one in question, his mind, with surprising recall, began to rifle through the sequential panels on the pertinent page of *Detective Comics*. **Panel one**: Batman feeling around for screws in the corners of the coffin. **Panel two**: Batman's gloved hand fumbling to find something on his utility belt. **Panel three**: Batman extracting a tiny screwdriver from said utility belt. **Panel four**: Batman dislodging the wooden panel that was behind the crown of his head. **Panel five**: Batman using the dislodged wooden panel as his shovel and digging his way up to freedom, lickety-split!

It was quite a satisfying solution, if Harry did say so himself, but not an easy one. Harry, as he well knew, was no Batman, nor was he in the habit of carrying around a tiny screwdriver, or even a normal-sized screwdriver for that matter, but he figured he could worry about that once he found some actual screws. So, methodically, he began to slide his hands over the wood, searching for whatever fasteners had been used to construct it. His fingers found the spot where the lid joined the sides, and he slowly slid his fingers along until they reached the back of the coffin. He then started to work his way down the panel behind his head, until he reached the point where it connected to the floor. But along the way, he found nothing—no screws, no nails, no latches—but then, just as he started to pull his hands away from the panel, he *did* brush up against *something*. In fact, two somethings—two objects that were resting on the floor an inch or two above his head. With each hand, he grasped them—one was round, the other cylindrical—and he pulled them forward so that they were inches from his face. And, although he could see nothing in the darkness, he still stared hard into the space where he knew they hovered, and somehow that effort allowed his hands to decipher what they were holding.

"An apple," he said. "An apple...and a bottle of water. But how?"

So stunned was Harry by this discovery that he went dead silent after that, almost as if he was listening for a response.

And then one came.

2

The borehole was intended only for the purpose of sending down food, water and oxygen; it was never meant for communication.

When Harry woke up in the coffin, Bethany had been up in her bedroom, getting ready for a night out with the girls. While she'd carefully applied her make-up and relished the act of brushing her long auburn hair, she missed all of the action down below—all of the screaming and blubbering. And when she finally did go downstairs (only after she'd modeled no less than three outfits in her full-length mirror), and descended further into the basement to send down an apple and a bottle of water to Harry, the only sound she heard coming up from the coffin was him going, "Come on, you silly bugger. Go down! Go down! There's only so much room in here for the two of us!"

Bethany was bewildered, to say the least.

"Has he already gone crazy?" she wondered. "Does he really think there's someone else down in there with him?"

It seemed impossible. Harry might've been weak-minded (and of that, Bethany had very little doubt), but she still couldn't believe that he'd completely fallen apart after less than twenty-four hours underground. Not even Harry was that pathetic.

Crouching down as quietly as she could, Bethany listened for further evidence of his mental decline, but there was none... Harry had suddenly gone silent. As she hovered just inches above the mouth of the borehole (careful not to touch her knees to the floor and risk smudging her brand new burgundy jeans), she heard neither sound nor movement. She held her breath for several more seconds and listened intently, before daring to slip the apple and a bottle of water from her purse and ease them into the hole. And as she released them, her whole body tensed, expecting their clatter to alert Harry to her presence six feet above him, but their plummet was mercifully muffled, and Harry's reaction was nonexistent.

It seemed she'd gotten away with it, and after a few more silent seconds, her body relaxed and a long, slow breath eased from her lips. Yet, just as she started to stand up, Harry's voice emerged from the grave, and a sensation like ice swelled in her stomach and spread throughout her veins.

"An apple," she heard him say. "An apple…and a bottle of water. But how?"

With all her might, Bethany tried to resist…tried her best to say nothing…tried to clamp her mouth shut and quietly stand up and tiptoe away, but, almost against her will, something still slipped from her lips.

"They're from me," she said, and the words sounded hollow and unfeeling, and she instantly regretted them.

To her surprise, there was no response—just the sound of rustling as Harry turned every which way inside the coffin, giving Bethany hope that she might still have time to escape. But then the rustling stopped, and in a desperate voice, Harry went, "Bethany?! Is that you?! Bethany?! Please answer me! I know I heard someone!"

Bethany bit her lip. Her mind was conflicted; she wanted to harden her heart and say nothing and walk away, but she could feel herself weaken. With a sigh, she said, "Yes, it's me."

"Oh, thank God!" Harry yelled.

"But look, Harry, I really can't talk right now."

"What?! What do you mean you can't talk right now?!"

"I mean what I mean. I shouldn't even be talking to you at all."

"What?!" Harry yelled, and Bethany sensed a tremor of panic start to stir inside of him. "You've got to get me out of here!"

"I told you I don't have time right now."

"Don't have time?! I'm buried alive! How can you not have the time!"

"Now look, Harry, I'm not going to argue with you! Do you hear me? I'm just not! I brought you some food and water, and I'll bring you more later. You're just going to have to be satisfied with that?"

"Satisfied with that?! Are you crazy?! I'm in a coffin, Bethany!"

"Harry, I'm serious now—I'm not going to talk to you at all if you insist on shouting." Bethany stood up and steeled herself to walk away. "Do you hear me, Harry?"

"Wait, Bethany, wait! Please!" The tremor of panic inside of Harry became a full on seismic event at the sound of her voice growing fainter after she stood up. "Okay, Bethany, I won't shout...I promise. I'm just a little worked up, that's all. I'm a little scared, you know. I admit it. But I'll stay calm, okay?" His voice was shaking all over. He took a deep breath and tried his best to settle it down. "But listen, honey, I need your help real bad. I need you to get me out of here, and then we've got to figure out how I got in here in the first place, okay?"

Bethany shook her head and rolled her eyes. "I'm not going to go into all of that. I'm just not. I'm not going to dredge up the past. I've got to move on with my life, Harry."

"Move on?!" Harry said, trying to remain calm but failing. "I'm in a coffin, buried underground! A few hours ago I was on the couch with my arm around you. That's not exactly ancient history!"

"I'm not going to go into all that, Harry. I'm just not."

"But Bethany—"

"But nothing! I brought you food and water, and I'll bring you more later, but that's it! I won't be bullied, Harry!"

"Bullied?!"

"That's right, bullied," Bethany snapped. "And now I've really got to go. I'm already late as it is."

"Go?! How can you go?! I'll die in here! What about me?!"

Bethany had already taken a step away, but stopped in her tracks. "You know, you have a lot of nerve saying 'What about you?' Are you serious? Is that really all you can think of? Yourself?"

"Well, I am the one who is buried alive, so..."

"I should've never even said a word to you!" Bethany shouted as she shook her head and angrily expelled air from her nose. "I should've just sent down the food and water like I planned and gone on with my life, but noooo, I'm too caring. That's always been my weakness. But not anymore! I wish you well, Harry...I really do...and I don't want to see anything bad happen to you, but I've got to move on. I can't be weighed down by your problems forever."

"My problems?!" Harry screeched. "What are you even talking about! My only problem is being buried alive, and that's a pretty real problem if you ask me!"

But, aside from the sound of her muffled footsteps growing fainter as she walked away, no response came.

"Wait, Bethany!" Harry screamed. "Bethany?! Please, no!!! Come back, Bethany! Oh my God, come back! I won't ask any more questions! Just get me out of here! That's all I care about! Just get me out! Please!!!"

Harry's screaming went on like that for quite some time, but Bethany only had to endure it for a few seconds more. She had ascended the basement stairs and gone out the front door, where she found her friends already parked alongside the curb, waiting for her.

And as her friends began to playfully honk their horn, thoughts of Harry began to quickly dissipate from her mind; and in fact, Harry would only enter her mind one more time that entire night, and even then, only briefly. After a long, whirlwind night of dancing and bar hopping and drinking and flirting, Bethany dozed in the backseat of the car as her friends drove her home, and it was then, somewhere between dreams and wakefulness, that she ever so briefly recalled Harry being entombed in her basement. But the recollection lasted only long enough for her groggy mind to come to a resolution: Not only would she no longer talk to him, but she would also not take him food or water. He was her past, and she decided then and there that she needed to completely move on.

From that point forward, Harry was dead to her.

3

The next morning, however, help *did come* to Harry in the form of a familiar voice. A man's voice.

"Harry? You down there, Harry? Watch your head, Harry. I'm sending down food."

A bottle of water rolled down into the crown of Harry's head, followed by a pear. Harry coughed twice and blinked into the darkness.

"Oh good, Harry, I hear you down there now. You had me a little worried there for a second, buddy."

"Warren?" Harry said. His voice was thick from sleep. "That you?"

"Yeah, you bet it's me," Warren said, and Harry could hear a smile in his voice.

"Well, where's Bethany?"

"Oh, you know..." Warren said, and Harry heard the smile in his voice falter. "You know how girls are. They're fickle. But don't let it worry you, pal. It's all good. The sun's still shining, ain't it?"

"I wouldn't know, Warren," Harry said.

"Oh yeah, my bad—sorry about that. But it is, Harry...it is. You're just going to have to trust me on that one."

"I do trust you, Warren," Harry said. "But if you could get me out of here, I wouldn't have to trust you on it. I could see it for myself."

"Yeah, well....that," Warren said, and Harry knew he was making the face he always made when Bethany asked him something he didn't want to answer. "You see, I told

Bethany I'd help out with sending food and water down to you, and, you know, keeping you company while she's busy...'cause she's really busy right now, you know, Harry...but she and I never really discussed anything about getting you out. So, I just don't know. I mean, it puts me in a tough spot, see."

"Not as tough as my spot," Harry said.

"Oh now, don't be like that. I'm here for you. I really am! It's just...well, you know how Bethany can be. I mean, let's face it—she's spoiled. And that's as much my fault as anyone's. But it is what it is, right?"

Harry said nothing. He wanted to scream.

"But look, I love her, and you love her," Warren said. "So, we're going to respect her wishes on this, even though I know that's not easy for you."

Harry was silent for a long time. So long, in fact, that Warren was just about to ask him if he was alright, when Harry finally said, "All I want to know is why. Why did she do this to me?"

"Well," Warren said, "I mean, I think she's just a little confused right now, you know. But aren't we all?"

"Confused about what?" Harry's voice was flat and lifeless.

"Well, frankly, confused about you."

"About me?"

"Yeah, you," Warren said, and then after a pause, he added, "And about me, too. Us, really."

"Us?"

"Yes, us."

For a moment, Harry felt like the bottom of the coffin

had collapsed and he was plummeting toward the center of the earth, and as he fell, his mind began to sputter, like it was on the verge of shorting out altogether, but then it righted itself, and strange and confusing images began to emerge from it. He saw Harry Houdini, illuminated by moonlight, in form-fitting cargo shorts that tightened around his muscular legs. And he saw Batman, shirtless, his wavy hair wafting in the breeze. And Robin, his boy wonder, nude, muscular and tangled up in heavy chains. When the feeling of falling finally abated, and Harry's body shuddered as if it had landed with a thud, a final image appeared in his mind's eye: Warren, smiling his boyish, effervescent smile, as his deep blue eyes shone below his shock of wavy hair.

" Do you know what love is, Harry?" Warren said.

"I don't know," Harry stammered. "Maybe."

"Love is when you not only see yourself in someone else, but also when you see a greater version of yourself in them."

Harry was quiet for a moment and then said, "I'm not sure I understand."

"I think you do understand," Warren said. "You just haven't let yourself yet."

Harry coughed and his eyes began to water as an image of Houdini flashed through his mind, underwater, bound in chains, struggling to free himself, but failing.

"Listen, buddy," Warren said, "I've got to get going, but I'll be back. I promise. You just hang tight in there, alright? We'll figure something out, okay?"

Harry didn't say anything. He blinked in the darkness, loosening the tears to roll down his cheeks.

4

When you're buried alive, as you may know from experience, you reach a point (much sooner than you might expect) where you lose track of time. Such was the case with Harry.

As he lay there in the musty darkness, trying to piece it all back together, he couldn't get all of the pieces to fit. He couldn't figure out how long he'd been down there, or how long it'd been since Bethany's one and only visit, or even how much time had elapsed between her visit and Warren's. Logically, he knew it couldn't have been more than two, maybe three days, but it felt much longer. It felt like months, or even years, or maybe even a lifetime...almost as if he'd *been born buried alive,* and all his memories of sunlight and the sky and other people were nothing more than the stuff of dreams.

Yet, he knew (or at least felt he knew) that he *couldn't possibly* have been born into such a circumstance, but must have been put down there by Bethany.

"Didn't she admit as much?" Harry thought, but then began to wonder, "Or did she?"

Wracking his brain, he tried to think back to their conversation, but found it hard to recall in detail. The occasional phrase came back to him ("You know, you have a lot of nerve saying 'What about you?'" and "I can't be weighed down by your problems forever."), but for the most part, their conversation seemed like a blur of her saying over and over that she wasn't going to discuss it. Like it or not, Harry had to admit to himself that, although Bethany clearly had some knowledge of how he ended up in the ground, he couldn't specifically recall her admitting to putting him there.

Harry then turned his thoughts to Warren.

"Surely, he had admitted that it was Bethany who had buried me?" he thought. Yet, exactly like when he'd tried to recall his conversation with Bethany, he found that his recollection of his conversation with Warren didn't produce a smoking gun. Exactly like Bethany, Warren had tiptoed around the topic, but had never explicitly said who was guilty.

"But it *had* to have been her," Harry thought, and immediately began to wonder how he could've ever loved someone like her...someone so selfish and cold-hearted.

"It's like Warren said," Harry thought, "love is when you see yourself in someone else, *and* when you also see a better version of yourself in them. I didn't have either with Bethany, did I? It's not like she just became cold-hearted; she always was. So, then, why in the world was I with her in the first place?"

Harry tried to come up with an answer to his own question, but every time one began to come together, it would as quickly start to crumble apart, so that the answer remained just beyond his comprehension, until, finally, the meaning of the question he was trying to answer began to crumble too.

Then there was just darkness. Darkness, followed by the quiet murmur of his snores.

5

Sleep can often be a sweet relief, and even sweeter when filled with comforting dreams. Harry, more than anyone, needed such sweetness.

Cradled in the soft arms of slumber, Harry dreamed that he'd been awoken by the sound of Warren's voice—"Hey, buddy, you over there?"—but the voice, although muffled, was closer than it had been when they spoke through six feet of earth. He felt Warren's touch—his warm hand against his own hand—and he realized Warren was buried next to him, and a small hole in the sides of their coffins allowed their hands to meet.

"Oh my God," Harry said. "How'd you get down here?" He was squeezing Warren's hand inside his own.

"Well, you know," Warren said, "I figured it was the least I could do."

Inside his own hand, Warren's felt so big and strong and kind. Harry could feel it's warmth spreading over his entire body, cradling him...caressing him.

"Does Bethany know you're down here?" Harry said, and he felt a chill of fear begin to emerge inside him, but then the warmth from Warren's hand caused it to melt away.

"Doubt it," Warren said. "I mean, really, when you think about it, we didn't even realize we were down here ourselves until just now."

Harry wasn't sure what Warren meant by that, but felt he believed it anyway. For, somehow, his heart knew it to be true.

6

"Oh yeah, right, the Fourth of July."

That was Harry's first thought when he woke up. It was the muffled sound of *bang-bang-bang* that had awakened him.

His next thought was of Warren; their hands coupled together; their heads lolling toward one another through coffin walls.

After that, he thought: "Coffin, then bed?"

Harry squinted hard against the glaring white lights. His eyes were brimming with tears and sweat, and everything was a blur. Gradually, the shape of a figure began to emerge from the haze of whiteness before him. It was Warren, standing over him; his face, too, moist with perspiration. He was shirtless, and he began to briskly smack his hand against the headboard: *Bang-bang-bang*!

Blinking sweat from his eyes, Harry quickly scanned the length of his own nearly nude body lying upon a tangle of pure white sheets. He moved—or at least tried to—but every muscle in his body was stiff; the slightest movement caused an ache to crawl up into him from the marrow of his bones. For the moment, he gave up on movement.

Allowing his body to slacken into the mattress, he looked up at Warren, fixing his gaze upon his deep blue eyes. "How? How'd you ever manage to get me out?".

"No time for that, Harry," Warren said. Harry now noticed there was a strange glint in Warren's eyes. A glint of fear.

"But—"

"No buts." With a firm grip, Warren grabbed Harry by the wrist and roughly jerked him up so that he was then seated on the bed.

"Owwwww," Harry cried out, as pins and needles resonated all up and down his back.

"Sorry about that, buddy, but you've got to go. Bethany could be home any minute."

Again, Harry felt himself being manhandled by Warren, and found himself precariously standing up on his jittery legs.

"What's it matter if Bethany comes home?"

"Trust me, it matters," Warren said. "Look, I mean it—you've got to go."

Warren tugged at him, frantically pulling Harry forward, while pushing him on the back, nearly causing Harry to tumble to his knees as he careened forward.

"Wait, Warren!" Harry called out, and stiffened so that he couldn't be so easily goaded. "Just wait one second, please!"

Warren kept his tight grip around Harry's wrist, but stopped pushing him. The desperate look in his eyes told Harry it was to be a short-lived reprieve.

"You—" Harry started to say, but stopped. He knew exactly what he wanted to say—knew exactly what he needed to say—but the words wanted to crawl back inside. As his eyes fell away from Warren, he found the courage to mutter, "You….could go with me."

Harry once again felt himself stumbling forward, as Warren hurried him across the bedroom

"Go! Go!" Warren shouted, and pushed Harry toward the door. But Harry stiffened and attempted to whirl around—to face Warren, to look into his eyes, even if for the last time—but his feeble legs failed; he stumbled sideways, trying to catch himself with an arm that was spinning madly in search of a surface.

"No! No! You've got to go! Now! Go! Go! Go!"

In a frenzy, Warren shoved Harry one more time...and that was all it took. Harry's hand did find a surface—the window sill—but only grazed it and skidded right by it; the momentum of his body carried him tumbling sideways, until he was crashing through the window and cascading through the air.

It was a strange feeling—being surrounded by a shower of shiny shards of glass and freely falling through the sky. And one would expect such a feeling to evoke fear... but Harry felt none. It wasn't that he didn't have time to feel it, because the fall—the actual plummet to the earth—was in slow motion. In fact, slow enough that Harry even had enough time to notice the very *absence of fear* and to wonder at the strangeness of it all.

Yet, being that it was such a beautiful day when Harry fell—bright and sunny and bathing his body in its warmth—maybe his lack of fear wasn't so strange after all. And, too, it certainly didn't hurt that he couldn't help but think of how very different this condition of falling was from that of mouldering in the grave. No more darkness, no more constraints, no more fear, nor shame.

His place, he knew then and forever, would be in the light. A light of clarity. An inner-light. A light that would cradle him, and protect him, so that if anyone—*even him-*

self—tried to bury him again, the earth would reject him. The light would see to that.

What We've Become

What a disaster that was. If I'd a been thinkin', I woulda called it off, but that was the whole problem—I *wasn't* thinkin'. But who could blame me?

One day I come home from work, and my wife of twenty-three years, who has never so much as changed her hairstyle in all that time, suddenly has poofy platinum blonde hair. Then, what seems like a day or two later, she starts runnin' around wearin' these business suit-type things. This is a lady who thought changin' from sweats to jeans was dressin' up, and now here she is lookin' like she's workin' on Wall Street. And when I asked what the deal was, she acted like, "What? I just got a few new things. Ain't I allowed to look nice?" So, okay, whatever, fine. But then I come home one night, and there she is sittin' on the couch, wearin' one of them suits and with her platinum hair all poofed up, and when she turns around to say hello to me, I see right away she don't look right, like maybe she's got too much make-up on, or like she's wearin' it different or somethin'…I dunno. But then she gets up and walks toward me, and even her walk is different. I mean, she kinda glides or strides or whatever you call it, like she's a runway model or somethin'. And that's when I see for sure that somethin' ain't right with her face. Somethin' ain't right at all. The lips are fuller, and the nose is smaller, and there's a beauty mark where there weren't one before, and I don't know what color her eyes used to be (I mean, I'm just not good at noticin' that sorta thing), but they sure as hell ain't the right color no more. That much I can see.

So, right then and there, I shoulda rung up Dale and Becky and said, "We ain't playin' cards tonight. We maybe ain't ever playin' cards again." But I didn't. I was too in shock. And not just about how my wife had changed, but about what she said when I finally went, "Erin, what the hell is goin' on with you? First the hair, then the suits...and now, what the hell you gone and done to your face?" And you know what she said? You know what she had the gall to say to me? "Nothin'." That's what she said: "Nothin." Can you believe that? And no matter how much I argued — because believe me, I argued 'til my face was as purple as a plum — all she'd say was that I was crazy; that my imagination was gettin' carried away; that nothin' had changed. Nothin'.

It was right about then — right after I'd argued myself crazy — that the doorbell rung. So, you can just about imagine what went through my mind when I heard that. I'd completely forgotten about Dale and Becky — I mean, *completely*. So, there I was, havin' practically pulled every hair outta my head over this mess, and the doorbell starts ringin' all ching-chime-chummy. And I tell ya what — I'd a been happier to see two Jehovah Witnesses than I was to see those two at my door. But what could I do? Turn out the lights and act like we wasn't there? It was too late for that game. I just had to put on a false face and make the best of it. What else could be done?

So, I open the door, and Dale and Becky come barrelin' in like gangbusters, carryin' a six a beer and a bottle a wine and pattin' my back and shakin' my hand like a couple maniacs. So, I knew then and there they was already half in the bag. But what's new? Couple a alcoholics like them, they no doubt had some drinks with dinner, then stopped off for drinks on the way over, and knowin' Dale, he probably had a couple on the drive too. But I put on a good show for 'em. I whooped it up like I'd never been happier to see two people in my whole goddamn life, and we all laughed like hyenas at everything each other said, while we made our way into the dining room where we always play cards.

So, I'll spare you a play-by-play of the whole night, and just skip to the important part, which is that Dale and Becky acted like nothin' was wrong. Like everything was normal. Like everything was hunky-dory. I mean, the entire night, they played cards, they laughed, they talked, they drank, and never once did they let on that they could tell Erin didn't look a damn thing like herself. So, finally, Erin goes to the bathroom, and by that point I'm pretty drunk, but more important, I'm mad as a hornet that everyone's actin' like nothin' ain't wrong. But I try not to let my anger show—I try to keep my voice real steady—when I say to them, low enough that Erin can't hear, "Ain't you noticed somethin' different about Erin?"

But they weren't givin' up the charade that easy. They gave me a look like they ain't got the slightest idea what I'm talkin' about, and then Becky has the nerve to go, "Different?"

So, real slow, like I'm talkin' to someone stupid, I go, "Yeah, different. Like her hair and her dress and her face. You know, different." And when I get to the last word, I'm practically shoutin', and my voice is shakin' all over the place, but there's nothin' I can do about it by then.

But Dale and Becky don't seem to notice, because instead of tryin' to kinda calm things down, they start makin' faces at each other like they have no idea what I'm talkin' about, and then Dale goes, "I don't notice anything different at all. Why—she get her hair done or something?"

And that's when I go through the roof. I can't tell ya what I said, 'cause I don't even remember...that's how mad I was. All I know is I was seein' red, and words were just jumpin' outta my mouth. And they must've been some pretty salty words too, because...well, you ever yell at a dog—maybe even give it a kick in the ass—and it has no idea why? You know that look it gives before it sulks away? That's the look Dale and Becky had the whole time, even up to the last second when I chased them out and slammed the front door right in their faces.

"And don't ever come back!" I yelled over the sound of the door. Then I turned around, with my eyes still full've red, and realized Erin was back from the bathroom, standin' there with her mouth hangin' open, and her face a mixture of disgust and confusion and anger and probably a few other things too.

But it didn't matter what expression it had on it—it still weren't her normal face. Not even close.

****

So, that night Erin doesn't want me to sleep with her, which is fine by me, 'cause I didn't want to sleep with no stranger in the bed next to me anyway. So, I end up on the couch, and I don't even have a blanket, and the only pillow I have is one of the couch pillows...the lumpy one, not the one that feels like a brick. But who cares at that point, really?

But even out there on the couch, it still felt weird knowin' that in the room right above me, some stranger was sleepin' in the bed where my wife shoulda been. I mean, I wasn't scared or nothin', but it still felt like, how can I go to sleep with a stranger in my house? But even more than that—I mean, once the anger had simmered down—I just felt real sad and confused.

I mean, what happened? Twenty-three years of everything being normal...of everything being good...and then this. I mean, me and Erin, we was meant for each other. We was pretty much two peas in a pod. I mean, we both liked playin' cards, and havin' drinks, and goin' bowling, and watchin' racing. But even more than that, we just saw things the same way. I mean, the kinda people I didn't like were the same kinda people she didn't like, and the kinda people I did like were the same kinda people she liked. Just regular folks. Down-to-earth, normal people. Like Dale and Becky, I thought, and felt even sadder and more than a little embarrassed.

I rolled over on my side away from the window, 'cause the streetlight out front was shinin' to beat the band, and I punched at the lumpy pillow, tryin' to get the lumps to spread out enough so that I could get my head down between 'em. I tried to close my eyes, but they just popped back open without me even realizin' it. I mean, I'd think I was tryin' to fall asleep—think my eyes *were shut*—but then realize my eyes were wide open and just starin' at the back of the couch. Then I'd lay there just feelin' my heart thumpin' inside my ribs.

Then I'd flip over on my other side, and look at how all the shadows in the room had a kinda orange-ish glow to 'em, and how nothin' in there quite looked like itself. I mean, I could tell what everything was—I knew the TV from the table from the La-Z-Boy—but they all looked a little different than normal, like it was me who was the stranger in the house. Like this house weren't even mine...like I hadn't lived here ever since me and Erin got married.

And to be completely honest—just to show you how messed up my head really was from it all—it kinda felt like I didn't even know where I was. I mean, not even what state I was in, or what country, or even planet. Least that's the sorta stuff that was swirlin' 'round in my head before I finally did fall asleep, without even realizin' I'd closed my eyes.

****

I got maybe two hours a sleep. And when I came to the next morning—the orange streetlight and the shadows were gone, and the room was filled with sunlight. Everything looked normal again.

I swung my feet to the floor and set up. I put my elbows on my knees and my face in my hands. I felt hungover—even more than I should've—and my body ached. I mean, when I stood up, my knees was like rusty metal grindin' against each other, and a sharp pain ran all up and down my spine.

Squintin' into the sunlight, I started trudgin' toward the kitchen. It was gonna take a lot of coffee to lift this fog. But then I heard somethin' comin' from the dining room—it might've been a voice, or maybe just the sound of a fork against a plate, but it was enough to stop me in my tracks.

Standin' perfectly still, I listened, figurin' it might be Erin. Because if it was, I wanted to know about it. I wanted to get my thoughts together and brace myself before seein' her. But then I heard another sound…the sound of laughter…a fella and a gal's. So, I turned and headed straight for the dining room where it come from.

When I walked in, I couldn't believe what I saw. The table was chock full've breakfast foods and plates and whatnot, and three people was sittin' around it…and I didn't recognize a one of 'em. Least not right away. But they was all lookin' at me—a fella and two gals—all smilin' to beat the band and waitin', like soon as I said somethin we was all gonna have a good laugh. But I didn't say a word. Nothin'… not a peep. My eyes just kept switchin' from one person to the next, lookin' at their teeth and hair and clothes, and not recognizin' none of it…until the one gal finally started to say somethin'.

Just as her lips parted, I seen something…I don't even know what it was…maybe just a crease near the edge of her lips…maybe just the shape of a tooth…maybe even just some saliva…I dunno…somethin' that makes me realize it's Erin.

"Isn't this a surprise?" she goes.

And I think, "You can sure say that again," because not only is her poofy platinum hair and business suit gone, but her whole face is now completely different than it was even the night before.

I try to say somethin'—my mouth even flops open—but nothin' comes out. There ain't words for what I'm feelin'.

"Well, aren't you even going to say Hi to Dale and

Becky?" she goes.

And I look at the two others, and I know my face must be white as a sheet.

"I guess he's not too keen on people just dropping in," goes the fella.

And Erin goes, "Oh, you stop. Our two oldest friends are always welcome!"

Then the other gal gets in on the act and goes, "Who are you calling old?" And the three of them start laughin' like it was the best joke they'd ever heard.

Then when the laughter finally lets up, Erin goes, "Let me get you some coffee, honey." And as she walks away, she pretends to whisper to the others, "I think someone had a bit too much to drink last night, if you know what I mean," and they all crack up again, smilin' all around like this is the greatest day of their lives.

And I try to smile too. I try to look normal while I stand there, watchin' the back of a woman who looks nothin' like my wife, gettin' me a cup a coffee, the way a wife might do. And it dawns on me that not only do these people not look like who they are, but they're actin' like last night never even happened. Like I never flew off the handle...like I never kicked 'em outta my house and told 'em to stay out for good. I mean, there's no hard feelings. There's no funny looks. Like last night never even was.

So, Erin comes walkin' back toward me, holdin' a mug a coffee out my way, and I shit you not, she's already lookin' different again. Now she looks like somethin' out of a magazine. Not like a real wife, but like one of them wives in a magazine about homes and gardens or whatever. But I

reach out for the mug anyway, and I go, "Thank you," tryin'
to sound as normal as I can. But before the mug even touch-
es my hand, somethin' whooshes past Erin and hurls itself
into my legs, wrappin' it's arms around me so tight that my
knees almost buckle. And that gets everyone to laughin'
again...'cept me.

"Easy, honey," goes Erin.

And the other gal goes, "Looks like someone's daddy's
girl."

I look down and see two thin arms wrapped around me,
squeezin' me as tight as can be. And above them, all I see is
a messy mass a long brown hair. But then the head tilts, and
the little girl under all that hair turns her face up toward me
and shows me her big eyes, lookin' at me like I mean something to her...like I matter...like I have something to offer.
But I know I don't. Yet, when she lets go a one of my legs
and reaches up with her small hand, I reach down and take
it inside mine, without even thinkin'.

"C'mere, Daddy, I wanna show you something," she
goes, and I hear both gals go, "Awww," but I don't see 'em,
'cause everything around me is just a blur of light then,
'cept for the little girl...she's crystal clear.

So, I let her lead me from the dining room to the back-
room, but while we're walkin', I'm thinkin', "But I don't
even have a daughter...I've never had one. Never even
wanted one." Yet, I don't hesitate at all. Even in the back-
room, when she takes me into the closet, I just go along with
her like it's all fine. Like it's all normal.

Then we go out the other side of the closet and into a
room I didn't even know we had. A room filled with white

sunlight and windows covered in white drapes and a small round table covered in a white tablecloth. The table is set for tea with a toy tea set, and around it are four chairs. Two with stuffed animals in 'em—a pink bunny and a gray kitty—and two that don't have nothin' in 'em.

"Isn't it beautiful, Daddy?" goes the girl, as she takes me over to one of the chairs.

"It is," I go, and sit down.

She sits down in the other chair and starts pretendin' to pour us out some tea from the toy teapot. She's pourin' for all of us, includin' the bunny and the kitty. And I watch her face—her big eyes that believe in everything they see—and I see how serious she takes it all, like she's doin' somethin' they taught her in church. And when she's done, she's real careful to put the teapot right back where it was.

Then she offers me some invisible cookies from a toy plate. I take a couple—real careful to open my hand just the right size for a couple cookies—and I put 'em on a little plate. Then I lift the tea cup, puttin' it close to my lips, and I blow on it real gentle-like, so as to cool it, but not to blow any outta the cup. Then, real careful, I sip at it, and while I sip at it, I watch her, and she watches me. Then she sips too.

"Good, huh?" she says.

"It is," I go.

"Try the cookies," she goes, and I do.

"They're good too."

She nibbles at her cookies and nods.

And it's right then—right at that moment—that I realize that for the first time in weeks (maybe months, or even years) I feel calm. Sittin' in this white room, eatin' imaginary food with a little girl I don't know—but who says she's my daughter—I feel like everything is okay, even if it isn't.

"You want me to go get Mommy?" she goes, and I feel myself start to shake my head "No", but then I don't.

I picture the gal in the other room—the gal named Erin; the gal who is my wife—and I realize that when I see her again, she'll be different than the last time I saw her, and the next time I see her after that, she'll be different again.

I reach out across the table. My daughter puts her little hand inside of mine.

"Yes," I say.

Your Soul to Keep

The only thing worse than monotony is monotony you have to work at. That's how the tube is.

You have to work at the others too—the bellows and the electrode pads—but not as hard as the tube. With the others, you can sometimes let your mind drift; you can forget the monotony from time to time. But not with the tube. Not if you want to live, that is.

I place one end of the flexible tube in my mouth, like I do at the top of every waking hour, and I press the other end of the tube to my sternum. As I was taught long ago, I inhale deeply, then exhale with force, but not so much force that the tube is ejected from my mouth. Then I repeat: inhale, exhale, inhale, exhale, for the next twenty minutes. It is all I can think about until I am done.

Many years ago, I used to think about the good it was doing me. That was some distraction at least, and more than a little comfort. I used to concentrate, trying to feel the difference it was making, trying to feel my lungs working better. But nothing seemed to change. I never detected even the slightest difference, and after a while, I quit trying to.

A couple minutes pass before the Keeper enters to give me the hourly report. It is difficult to hear her over the sound of my own breathing and through the thick plastic shield that covers her head. But what she says is almost identical to what she always says, hour after hour, day after day.

"Thank goodness," she goes, "I was so worried you'd forget. But you never forget, do you? You're a good boy." She draws closer and raises her heavily gloved hand toward my face, but then thinks better of it, lowering her hand for fear that one of us might inadvertently cause harm to the other. She then gives her report, and I look at the window, or rather at the single opaque shade pulled down over it.

"Storms are raging," the Keeper goes. "The sky is jet black, except for when lightning bolts fissure it. Strong winds are tearing trees from the ground. Hail is damaging every surface in sight. In the distance, we hear the detonation of bombs. They are drawing nearer, and soon we will see the fires and hear the anguished cries of those injured by them. Animals—or are they men?—roam the streets in packs, searching for food. No living thing is taboo. They kill everything they touch, leaving only bones and misery in their wake."

The report is over. The Keeper suddenly seems exhausted. Having used all of her allotted time, she reaches out for me again, but then quickly exits before making contact. Only then do my eyes fall away from the window.

After I finish the tube, I begin the bellows. I place the nozzle to my sternum and take the handles in my hands. I press the handles together, and the bellows emit a stream of air. I then pull the handles apart, and repeat. It is for my heart. It keeps it from dying.

While doing it, I become like a machine. It takes less concentration than the tube, so my mind is able to wander. I stare at the opaque shade over the window and think about the Keeper, because lately I have begun to think that what she is reporting is not something she has seen firsthand. Instead, I suspect she is in a room just like I am, and her reports are coming from reports that are given to her. Hourly, I assume...probably from another Keeper. I don't know this to be a fact. It is purely a hunch. But it is a hunch that feels more and more real with each passing day.

After twenty minutes elapse, I switch to the electrode pads. I put my hands behind my back and press the pads to my kidneys, and I watch the window, and I wonder. If the reports are being passed from Keeper to Keeper, who is the Keeper at the front of the line, and why does the line end with me? Is it possible that there isn't even a front to the line? Could all the reports somehow be secondhand, or worse still, entirely fabricated?

I finish with the electrode pads. I put them away. I get the tube. I then look at the opaque shade over the window, and I pause just before placing the tube in my mouth. Never—not once—have I seen for myself what is beyond that shade. I know only what I am told.

I take two steps toward it. The Keeper will be here soon, and I am endangering myself by not using the tube, so I concentrate for a moment, trying to feel if my lungs are slowly collapsing...slowly shriveling and dying. But I feel nothing. My breaths come neither easier nor harder than before. With as much concentration as I can muster, I listen. Is there a rattling in my chest? A wheezing? Any sign—no matter how slight—that my lungs are beginning to fail? But I hear nothing.

I take two more steps toward the window, so that I am close enough now to touch the shade. I listen again. I hear nothing within me other than healthy breaths. But beyond the shade—beyond the window—I think that I hear the muffled sound of bombs. Or was that thunder? But then I realize, I am only hearing my own fearful heartbeats throbbing in my ears.

I reach out my hand. My fingertips lightly touch the shade and slide down until they reach the bottom. I grab it and lift it, and at that exact moment, I hear behind me the sound of the Keeper entering the room. But then there is silence...silence in the room *and beyond it,* and I wonder if she sees the same thing I am seeing. First, a jet black sky and a dead Earth. But then, as my mind catches up with my eyes, a blue sky, a green Earth, and a single majestic tree with branches stretching out in every direction, like the mighty arms of a many-limbed god.

Behind me, I hear footsteps approaching. I continue to hold the shade up. The tube falls from my hand.

The Miraculous

Listen, friend, I appreciate you stoppin on this bitter cold night and being so generous. Lemme just see what it was you gimme. Look like a dollar, two case quarters and three pennies...one of em wheat. Must be my lucky day...I get to eat.

But listen, friend, I know you's in a hurry...I see you's all dressed up with places to go and people to meet...but lemme just shake your hand before you go. I know you wanna get out the cold, and Lord knows I wish I could too, but lemme just shake your generous hand real quick and share a little somethin with you to show my appreciation. It won't take but a minute, really. And what's a minute in the grand scheme a things? It ain't nothin. A minute ain't even a second in the grand scheme.

But now listen, I know you's a good person—you might even be a saint for all I know—but I still gotta warn you that this is some tip-tip-tiptop secret stuff I'm bout to let you in on, okay? I mean the tippest most of the toppest most, okay? So, you can't say sugar to nobody about it, you hear? Cause this is somethin I learned from a buddy a mine that used to work down there at NASA. Now I can't tell you his name, so don't even ask me. I mean, *I know his name*, cause he was my buddy, but I just can't go tellin you what it was. That's classified, see. Purely on a need to know basis. And trust me, you don't wanna need to know. You don't wanna get too deep into this, the way I am. But you *do need to know* at least the basics, just so you's aware. Just so's you know everything ain't always as it seems.

So, lemme lay it on you—but you may wanna brace yourself first, cause this is some heavy-duty stuff. It all

started when my buddy was in the laboratory with a bunch
of them NASA scientists, all lookin through one of them
high-powered telescopes that's so strong it could spot a
mosquito on Mars. But it weren't no mosquito they spotted,
and it weren't on no Mars neither. Cause you know what
it was? A boy! A real live human boy runnin wild on the
surface of the moon! You hear what I'm tellin you? A boy!
And it was a pitiful sight too, my buddy said. No more than
eight years old, all alone, dressed in rags, just a'runnin on
the surface of the moon like some kinda wild animal. Which
I spose he was, when you think about it. Like some kinda rat, just a'followin every little whim of his animal mind,
which had probably done shrunk down to about the size of
a walnut by then through evil-lution and whatnot.

　　Now, I know what you's thinkin—you don't even have
to say a word—cause I was thinkin it too. I was thinkin,
how in the world does a boy end up on the moon? Well,
my buddy said the way them scientists figured it was that
there musta been a whole family of em up there at one time,
but when they up and left, the boy got left behind. Abandoned, you could say. But sad as that is—and it's about as
sad as sad gets—them scientists told my buddy that it's still
a woman's right to abandon her own child on the moon.
And who am I to argue with that? I mean, that's science!
You can't argue with no science! And when you think about
it, it's like my buddy also said—it ain't really the govern-
ment's problem neither. They need to keep they nose out
of it! It ain't taxpayer money that should be spent on savin
abandoned children on the moon! I mean, the boy survived
this long on his own, didn't he? He just gonna have to sur-

vive a little longer and pull up his bootstraps and find his own darn way down to Earth!

But I tell you what though...it's still sad as sad gets, don't you think? I mean, I get a lump in my throat just a'thinkin about it. Just imaginin that little rat-boy all alone, runnin scared out there in space.

Wait, wait! Please don't go yet! Don't walk away all full of tears and sadness. Lemme tell you something happy before you go. Somethin that will lift your spirits and put a smile on your face, okay? I know it's cold, but lemme just tell you this one thing. It'll just take a second. Please...

Oh, thank you, thank you, thank you...you won't be sorry. Trust me. You gonna like this.

This all happened about a month after my buddy saw that rat-boy on the moon I was just tellin you bout, which, not coincidentally, was bout a month after my buddy was fired from NASA without rhyme nor reason. I mean, they said it was about him stealin them space pens...you know, the ones that write upside-down. But that ain't no reason. That's what you call an excuse, not a reason.

Huh? Oh yeah, yeah, I'll get on with it. Sure, sure. I know you's busy. Night out on the town, dressed to kill...I got you. You ain't gotta tell me twice.

So, where was I? Oh yeah...this all went down in a motel room where this weird lookin guy with a head like a lumpy potato asked me and my buddy to go. Said he wanted us to see something. Said it was a rare treat, and boy, he weren't lying.

So, me, my buddy and Mr. Potato Head squeeze into this tiny motel bathroom, but it ain't just us, cause there's this lady in there too, sittin in a wooden chair, wearin only a bra and panties and with a few motel towels draped over her shoulders and lap. But it ain't what you think, trust me. It's weirder...weirder by a country mile.

Now, Mr. Potato Head's got this real screechy voice, see...screechy like a screech owl's...and he starts going, "In days of yore, my good people, trepanation released spirits..." and that's when I noticed he got a hand drill in his hand, and he keeps screechin on like, "But in these modern times, that is...this great century of ours!...with skyscrapers and such... and computers...and high-tech toothbrushes... and electric razors and what have you...um...in this modern world of ours...science tells us the benefits are...well...more scientific! Including, increasin blood in the brain and makin more brain space...more volume!...more oxygen!...and a higher state of consciousness, see...and blood!... and psychic powers...and even more blood!"

And that's when the girl commences to screamin for him to wait, and I was bout to start screamin right along with her, but it was too late for all that, cause it was right about then when that nasty drill bit ripped clean through her skull. And there weren't no sound of crunchin bone neither, cause that drill done drowned it all out. And there weren't even that much blood neither...just some little sputtering pink bubbles and, like, a drool. But then the drill slipped from Mr. Potato Head's hand and sunk clean down into the center of that poor lady's brain.

You wanna talk about blood? I'll tell you bout blood. When he yanked that drill back out, there sho'nuff was blood! Blood shootin clean up to the ceiling, like it come out a hose, and at the same time sprayin everything in sight like one a them there rotating sprinkler heads. It was a rare sight, indeed. No two ways about it.

Oh, please wait, you're gonna miss the best part if you go now! The important part! The part that's gonna make you so happy! Please just wait another second...I swear you're gonna wanna hear this, cause it's like a miracle. And tell me, when you last heard about a genuine miracle, huh? Oh, please don't look at me like that. I'm sorry about the coat...I didn't mean to grab it and ruffle your feathers. I just got excited, that's all. On account of the miracle. The one I'm gonna tell you about if you just give me another second. Just one more second, okay?

See, I knew you was a good person! The second you stopped on this bitter cold day and said lemme give this wretched man a dollar and fifty-three cent, I knew I was in the presence of a saint. A real live walkin the Earth saint!

Okay, okay, I see you lookin at me...so here's the happy part. Here's what you been waitin for. As it turns out, that poor lady whose brains got all turned to creamed corn in that motel room survived. You hear what I'm sayin? She lived! *Now, that right there is a miracle in and of itself*...but that ain't the miracle I'm bout to tell you about! Cause what happened was that there was somethin bout the way her brains got all swirled up inside her head that gave her all the benefits of trepanation that Mr. Potato Head was talkin bout and then some! Psychic powers, second sight, proba- bly the ability to talk to ghosts...you name it, she got it! And it was these powers that helped her recall somethin she'd done buried deep down in her mind. Somethin she'd been tryin to forget for a long, long time. Somethin too painful for any woman...*any mother*...to remember. And I can tell by the way you's lookin at me that you know it too. And you know it's a true dyed-in-the-wool miracle!

That's right, she remembered the child she'd forgotten! Abandoned, you might say. That rat-boy up there in space all alone. He was hers! Her own flesh and blood! And I tell you, she sat there in that motel bathroom, with her brains all scrambled eggs, and tears just a'streamin down her face, and swore she'd get him back. Swore she'd save him! One way or the other she was gonna get back to that moon. And I don't doubt it neither. I don't doubt it one bit, what with her new-found powers and a mother's determination. Oh, happy day!

Wait, wait! Lemme just walk with you for a second. Boy, you's a real sprinter, ain't you? A real long strider. Lemme just catch up with you, but my legs ain't what they used to be, what with standin out in the elements all year round... out in the bitter cold and blazin sun...it can break a body down, you know. But listen, I just wanna thank you. I just wanna say what a saint you are, and how happy I am that I was able to bring a little light into your life too. And that ain't stuff I just share with anyone. That's some tip-tip-tip-top secret stuff, but I knew you could use it. I knew you'd tuck it away in your saintly heart, and use it out there in the world to do more good.

But hey, listen, just one more thing. You think maybe you could find it in your heart to spare me another forty-seven cent? You know, to take it up to an even two dollars? I mean, a dollar fifty-three ain't much to eat on. I mean...

Wait, wait! I can't run like that! You know I can't run! Wait, come back!

Shoot...

Oh well, maybe someone else'll come along and help me out. Just forty-seven more cent and I can get some eggs and coffee in me. Somethin to get me through another day. Some fuel.

Lord knows, miracles happen.

Just Desserts

The fact is, Di was waiting for death, but death kept delaying. In the meantime, she'd whittled her world down to three rooms: a bedroom, a bathroom and a kitchen; all three squalid and unlit. Since she didn't go out, a kindly neighbor brought in groceries a couple times a month. She never thanked him; never paid him. She survived on the sweets—cakes, pies, and cookies—and left the rest to the insects.

Di's gums were black; her teeth were nubs. Her legs were long thin vines, and her body was a pumpkin teetering precariously atop them. She could barely walk. Her bearings were capricious, and her knees had turned to rust and ash. A vast amount of her time was spent in bed alongside her only companion, a television set that endlessly blared.

Di had a recurring fantasy—it came from a movie she'd seen as a child, but had long since forgotten the name of. The fantasy was that she was in a canopy bed, and that death would come in the form of the canopy slowly lowering and painlessly smothering her in her sleep. The reality, however, was different. The reality was that life slowly smothered her; it covered her mouth and nostrils; it clogged up her throat and chest, and eventually, after many years, her whole being, until there was nothing left; no breath, no movement, nothing.

And yet, death still delayed.

****

Arriving with dew in the morning, a basket appeared outside Di's front door. Inside the basket, lying on a bed of dried grass, were some thin white pastries and a paper dunce cap. Glancing up and down the street, Di saw no one, so she whisked the basket up into her arms and ducked back inside her house.

Placing the basket on the table, she sat down and stared at the pastries. She could smell the scent of raw honey and confectioner's sugar rising from them, but when she took one in her hand, she saw the others were infested with black worms writhing about and burrowing into the white flesh of the pastries.

It occurred to her that it could be a callous prank—or even worse, a trap. Pushing back from the table, she stood up in disgust. She hobbled to the front door and out onto the porch.

"I know what you're tryin to do!" she croaked. She looked up and down the street through her rheumy eyes and strained her ears, but all was silent. "You ain't fooled me! I ain't taken a single bite, and never will!" She staggered back in and slammed the door behind her.

Standing by the table, she stared down at the pastries, watching the worms tunnel through them. She took the basket to the trash and let the pastries tumble in.

After some rummaging, she managed to find an old half-eaten piece of pie in the refrigerator. She devoured it— even going so far as to lift the plate to her face and lick it clean.

Hardly sated, she sat there trying hard not to think about the pastries in the trash behind her. She sat there for a long time. Then she put the paper dunce cap on and sat there some more. Still thinking.

****

Di was startled from her ruminations by a sharp knock at the door. "Wait! Wait!" she hollered as she hobbled toward it, but by time she got there, the person was gone, and only a basket remained. Inside the basket, lying on a plate of pristine white glass, was a chocolate cake. Glancing up and down the street, Di saw no one, so she whisked the basket into her arms and ducked back inside.

After placing the basket on the table, she stared at the cake, and could smell the rich scent of chocolate rising from it, and her mouth began to water. Yet, she remained suspicious. She feared the cake would be infested with worms. Tentatively, she touched the icing with her fingertip. It was soft and fresh; it stuck to her finger. She raised the finger to her nose and smelled it. The luscious scent set off sparks in her mind.

Di turned away from the cake and tottered toward the kitchen counter, where an assortment of unwashed utensils were spread out among towers of dirty dishes. She pawed the utensils, sending insects scattering in all directions, until a knife had been located, which she carried back to the table. Cutting the cake, she expected something inside it to impede the knife at any moment—a big rock, a hunk of rusty metal, a dead rat—but the knife went through it with ease. Making another cut—also without incident—she gently jiggled the piece of cake free. Once removed, it stood alone on the table before her, a thing of perfection.

Yet, Di remained cautious. Poking it with her finger, the cake proved to be moist and spongy. The residue it left on her skin gave off a delectable scent when held under her nose. Even when she positioned her finger inches from her eyes and examined the residue for the slightest intimation of foul play, there was nothing. It was merely cake...harmless cake.

Di put her finger to her tongue and wrapped her trembling lips around it. She slid her finger out and swallowed. She didn't move a muscle except to close her eyes and direct all of her attention toward her tongue. Her eyes opened, watery with emotion. The cake was not only safe, it was divine.

Di waddled back toward the kitchen counter, cursing herself all the way for not grabbing a fork the first time. By the time she got back to the table and plopped down, her breaths were ragged and sweat beaded on her forehead and upper lip. Her hand trembled as she touched the fork to the cake and sliced off a bite, but only a crumb or two was wasted on the return trip to her mouth.

The cake was heavenly. Scarcely had the first bite entered her mouth before she was already shoveling in another, and another after that, as the flavors erupted in her mouth and bathed her brain in pleasure. Within seconds, only a single bite remained.

Glassy-eyed and wearing a half-mustache of chocolate icing on her upper lip, Di scooped the last bite into her mouth, already making plans to devour a second slice. Yet, when she bit down, everything came to a halt. Her teeth collided with something that not only impeded her bite, but repelled it.

The fork fell clanging to the floor. Cupping a hand under her chin, she allowed a clump of masticated cake and viscous brown saliva to roll off her tongue and land wetly against her skin. Probing the gummy mess with her finger, she detected the culprit and clamped onto it. Then she recognized it for what it was.

She began to retch as her fingers involuntarily sprang apart, allowing the offending foreign body—a human tooth—to clatter to the floor.

****

A few moments passed before another sharp knock rattled the door. Di stiffened at the sound. Her chin was moist with thick brown drool, and a small puddle of vomit had pooled on the floor between her feet. She tried to call out, "Who's there?" but when she opened her mouth, the words caught in her throat from fear.

In silence, she waited, straining her ears to detect any hint of who was at the door. She desperately wanted to know who it was, but at the same time, was also afraid to find out. She imagined a faceless figure, coming to slit her throat, or a hooded man, coming to tie her up and torture her.

The heavy knock thundered against the door, and Di recoiled, almost falling over before her hands flattened against the tabletop and steadied her. Her breaths were shaky. She could feel her whole body trembling.

"Di?" said a voice beyond the door. "You in there, Di?"

She recognized the voice and felt relief—but also annoyance. It was Joe Gaskins, the neighbor who occasionally brought her groceries. Her instinct was to say nothing, to pretend she wasn't there, but he of all people knew she never left the house. He'd just keep knocking, or worse yet, call the police.

"I can't come to the door right now!" she yelled. "I'm busy!"

"Well, I've got some groceries for you, Di."

"Just leave em!"

"I can't. It's gonna rain. Just open up for a second."

"I can't. I'm naked!"

"Just open the door a crack and I'll slide em in and go. I won't look, I promise."

Di bared her teeth and let a hiss slowly escape. *He's like a damn tick the way he burrows in*, she thought. *Just like the whole damned world.*

Joe lightly knocked on the door again and said her name. Gritting her teeth, Di struggled to stand up. As she waddled toward the door, she called out, "What sweets you got in there?"

"Well, not too many, on account of your diabetes and all."

"Oh, I got the other kinda diabetes, not the kind where you gotta worry about it like that," she shouted, and then opened the door a few inches. "So, what do ya got?"

"Well, I got some fruit, and some crackers, and some bread, and some good — "

"No, I mean the sweets. What sweets you got in there?"

"Well, there's a pie..."

"A pie! What kind?" Di opened the door further.

"Cherry, I think."

"Gimmie that."

"Well, let me see if I can find it in here..." Joe said as he slowly searched around in the bag. "But while I'm lookin for it, I was wonderin if you'd had a chance to read them pamphlets I left for you yet? They're real important, you know."

"Oh, no, no, the print's too small on em," Di said as she impatiently watched him dig through the bag. "My eyes're too bad."

"But what about that magnifying glass I brought you?"

"Oh hell, I don't know where that's at. The roaches probably carried it off."

"Well, then, maybe I can just come in and read em to you sometime, or we can just read from the good book to-gether. I mean, you can't never go wrong doin that."

"Uh huh," Di said, and as soon as she glimpsed the pie rising out of the bag, she snatched it away from him.

"Maybe tomorrow then?" he said.

"Yeah, maybe."

"Really?"

Di ignored him. She held the pie under her nose and inhaled deeply.

"What do ya say, huh?" Joe said.

Di didn't even look up at him. She scurried backwards and slammed the door in his face, leaving Joe still holding the bag.

****

For the rest of the day and well into the night, there was not a single knock at her door. Lying in bed, Di enjoyed her pie in peace. Propping the dessert atop her amorphous breasts, she scooped out pieces with her fingers (which she thoroughly licked clean in between scoops), until it had been devoured. With her belly distended and crumbs clinging to her hair, she took a long succession of naps, while her TV blared in the background. With each gurgling snore that escaped from her sticky lips, her troubles seemed to recede further away.

Yet, as the black of night faded into the azure of dawn, Di was once again awakened by a sharp knock at the door. "Wait! Wait!" she hollered as she hobbled forward, but by time she got there, the person was gone and only a basket remained. Inside the basket, lying upon a soft white pillow, was a single sugar cookie...and next to it, a handgun. Glancing up and down the street, Di saw no one, so she whisked the basket up into her arms and ducked back inside.

Placing the basket on the table, she looked into it, and her eyes switched back and forth between its two offerings before gradually settling on one. Di had never fired a gun before; never even held one. Only once or twice had she even been near one, but those were guns for hunting, not handguns. Yet, as she gazed at the one below her, she felt drawn to it. She imagined picking it up; imagined the weight of it in her hand; the rough texture of its handle; the delicate resistance of its trigger against her finger. She could, if she cared to, put it to her temple. She could even put it in her mouth.

When she tried to reach for it, her hand froze, hovering in the air inches away, igniting a tremble in her fingertips that rippled up her arm and erupted into waves of fear in her body. Snatching her hand back as if she'd been burned, she held it against her breast, but continued to stare at the gun for a few more seconds with an expression of bewilderment upon her face.

Her eyes turned to the cookie. It was blonde, with a dusting of granulated sugar that was heavier toward the center than the edges. It was small and perfectly round—*almost too perfect*. Yet, she found it irresistible. Taking her trembling hand from her breast, she reached for the treat with caution, fearing she might accidentally brush up against the gun; and even after she had secured the cookie between her fingers, her movements remained guarded, and she kept one eye on the weapon, as if it might suddenly spring to life.

She lowered herself into the chair and took a moment to study the cookie, turning it over and tilting it side to side. She broke it in half and brought both pieces close to her nose. She laid one half down, and began to vigorously rub the other half between her fingers, causing it to crumble into tiny bits that descended onto the table. She examined the residue that remained on her fingertips. Everything checked out; the remnants looked fine; the cookie smelled delectable. Licking a finger, she pressed it into the cookie dust and then put the finger in her mouth. As she swallowed, her lips curved upward into a satisfied smile. Even in its adulterated form, the cookie was buttery and rich with vanilla, with just the right ratio of flour to sugar.

Within seconds, Di was licking all of her fingers at once. Then, her whole palm.

****

Di was still sitting at the table, but had fallen asleep, when she was startled awake by a sound. Not a knock at the door this time, but a voice. A familiar voice. The voice of Joe Gaskins—and it came from within the house.

When she raised her chin from her chest, her eyes blurred, and her thoughts sloshed around in her head like wet cement. Her body was heavy, and her arms hung limp at her sides. When she tried to focus her eyes, they criss-crossed, and nearly faded to black.

"You were sleepin," Joe said, and she could hear that he was close by.

"Eatin," she said, but it was hard to get the word out. Her lips were gluey, and her mouth felt funny, like her tongue was too big.

"No, I know the difference between sleepin and eatin, and you was definitely sleepin. But not no more. Now, you're awake. Not fully awake, mind you, but awake none-theless."

"Fully?"

"Yes, fully, unlike a fool."

Di could make out the blurry image of Joe sitting across from her, and she could hear his fingers lightly tapping on something as he spoke. She widened her eyes to see better, and when that didn't work, she squinted, and was able to discern that it was a big book on the table that he was tapping.

Aw, Christ, The Bible, she thought. *He's finally got me cornered like a rat.* But then she squinted harder, and a jolt of fear surged through her as she realized that the handgun was resting on top of the book.

"There used to be a time when neighbors looked out for one another," Joe said. "You didn't just have one kindly neighbor...they were all kindly. You know what I mean? Just think about the word 'neighborly'. What's it even mean nowadays, huh?"

Di looked from the gun to Joe and back to the gun. Her voice quivered as she said, "You've always been good to me, Joe."

"Well, sure I have been, but that's my point, ain't it? Who else could you a counted on to come here and do this?"

Di's mouth went bone dry, and she felt a lump in her throat. "What do you mean 'come here and do this'? Come here and do what?"

"Do what?" Joe said with a laugh. "Why, the very thing you been waitin' on, that's what. I mean, just imagine Ashley from across the street takin' the time to come over here and do this. Or what about Bruce Depree next door? Imagine Bruce findin time between his wife, his ex-wife and his mistress to come over here and help you out. Fat chance a that happening!"

Di nodded. Her eyes were still blurry, but she could see well enough to know that his hand had moved from the book to the gun, causing a thought to flash through her mind: maybe she could slide her hands under the table and flip it over. But the thought quickly withered away with the knowledge that she was far too weak to pull it off. She thought about running for the door, but that thought too was short-lived, as she knew she was far too slow to get away.

"I'm not askin for anyone's help," she said.

"A good neighbor don't wait to be asked," Joe said, and his finger slowly curled around the trigger. "You never asked me for groceries, but I still brung em, didn't I?"

"I know, Joe. You're a good man. I know you are."

"Aw, now..."

"But what I mean is I don't think I want what I wanted anymore."

Di's eyes searched the blurry face before her for some hint of understanding, but Joe just tilted his head to the side and stared at her, before he started chuckling. "Sounds to me like you don't know what you want."

"But I do, Joe, I do. I was just a little confused before, that's all."

"I'll say."

"But not anymore. I wanna live. I really do, Joe. You gotta believe me...I do!"

"Do you?"

"Yes."

"Or is it that you just don't wanna die?"

"Live, Joe, live!"

Joe lifted the gun from the book and sighed. "I don't believe it," he said, and pointed it at her.

Di threw her hands over her face and ducked. She started screaming, "No! No! I do! Please, Joe, you gotta believe me! I do!"

"Now, calm down. Hysterics ain't helpin no one."

"Please, please..."

"Now quiet down...I need you to listen."

"Please..."

"I'm serious now, shush. I need you to hear me, cause I

don't think you ever did really wanna die, try as you might."

"That's right...you're right..."

"No, it weren't death you wanted. It was you just wanted the hard parts of life to go away. Ain't that right?"

"Yes...yes..."

"Problem is, there ain't no such thing as a life without the hard parts," Joe said, and his chair gave a loud screech as he shoved it back across the floor and stood up.

"No! No!" Di screamed.

Joe stretched his arms out in front of him, putting both hands on the gun as he pointed it directly at her head. "So, now death has come, as it must, whether you want it to or not," Joe said; and Di wrapped her hands around the base of her skull and clamped her forearms tightly around her head. Tears were streaming down her cheeks. Her whole body was shaking.

"Please, please, please..."

"Look at you, beggin for a pardon. But for what? So that you can continue to deny life?"

"Please, Joe..."

"Look at me."

"No, no..."

"Look at me!"

Di flinched at the harsh sound of his voice, but then lowered her arm just enough to reveal one of her eyes.

"Look at me fully," Joe said, "unlike a fool."

"Please, Joe..."

"Shhhh," he said, and Di slowly lowered both arms and turned toward him. Her face was trembling, and she was blinking back tears.

"Stay with me," Joe said. "Don't close them eyes."

Di desperately wanted to look away—desperately wanted to close her eyes and imagine a white canopy slowly lowering onto her face and quietly taking her away, but she didn't. She raised her chin and set her quivering jaw as best she could, as she looked with both eyes into the reality of a gun barrel staring back at her like an unblinking eye, and in the blurriness behind it, two other eyes, watching her and deciding her fate.

"Now, you're alive," Joe said.

Di let out a sob, and Joe curled his finger around the trigger and pulled it.

A Soft Spot in the
Earth's Skull

1

Mother's windpipe in the bathtub. Trying to jam it down the drain with the handle of a wooden spoon, but it suddenly breaks like a crutch kicked out from under me. Mother's windpipe in the toilet whirling like an oversized worm in an undersized tornado, but it won't go down—it just keeps whirling.

Mother's windpipe on the stove next to a pot of leftover mac and cheese, a dusty tea kettle, some burnt crumbs, and stains that look like splattered spaghetti sauce or bloody wounds, depending on your mood.

In a frying pan coated in vegetable oil, mother's windpipe sizzles and crackles, still making a wicked noise like it always did.

On top of the trash in the kitchen, mother's tongue is silenced at last. It's like a dead slug on a dead leaf except the leaf is a frozen lasagna box not a leaf. As it dries out it becomes purple and white and the taste buds stand up stiffly. It feels like a cow's liver, and it left a stain on the lasagna box when I lifted it, but it slices up nicely on the wooden cutting board. You can make little cubes out of it, and long pieces, and thin pieces you can almost see through.

On the kitchen counter, in the ashtray, are mother's teeth and a half-spent Virginia Slim. Brown and yellow with rot, they are monkey teeth. They are dog teeth. They are ashy, and cigarette smoke twirls up from them as if from toppled buildings in a bombed-out city, or jagged stars, dislodged from the sky and fallen to the ground, extinguishing in the cool of the night.

2

Jeremy knew he wasn't really capable of killing his mother; he knew he didn't have the guts. But he thought about killing her an awful lot, and so he couldn't help but wonder why that was. Was it in hope that the fantasies would eventually become so great in number that they'd have no choice but to spill over into reality? Maybe...but Jeremy could never say for sure, because no matter how often he thought it through, he just got confused and never came to any real conclusion. Instead, after grinding the topic to a pulp in the gears of his mind, he would eventually wear out, and think, "The only thing I can say for sure about it all is that if the psychiatrists ever got a hold of me, they sure would have a field day."

But there was no chance of that happening, because Jeremy would never go within a thousand feet of a psychiatrist. The way he saw it was that no matter how confusing and troubling his fantasies were, there was still no way he was ever going to share them with someone else, including the so-called professionals.

Partly, that came down to shame. He could never share his secrets with a stranger. But even more than shame, it came down to fear. A fear of his mother finding out, because even though he was his own man—a man of fifty-three years, mind you—his mother still had her ways. He knew, deep in the pit of his stomach, that she'd find out one way or another, because she always did. It was almost like she could read his mind. Almost like she could look right into his dull gray eyes and see everything—even the very essence of his withered soul.

3

It began with a bowl of oatmeal and ended with a hole in the sky.

On a cheap, plastic tablecloth atop the kitchen table, steam twirled heavenward from a bowl. Next to it a colorless pear, cut into asymmetrical wedges, rested on a white saucer. In a white mug, stained with mauve lipstick, milky coffee grew cold while mother mocked her maker with a show of prayers.

A shaft of pale yellow light, swarming with dust motes, fell across and illuminated her hands, which were pressed together as if in supplication. Behind them, in the gloom, I could sense, but not see, her tongue—a bird's tongue—fat, black and pointed, darting between heavily made-up lips, as holy words were spat forth in an unholy rasp.

But that prayer shall remain forever unfinished. The hole the ball-peen hammer made in the back of her skull saw to that.

There was no resistance—the hammer tore through bone with ease, and as it slid back out, I could feel the shape of the hole left in its wake. The infinitesimal vibrations between bone and metal ran up the length of the hammer and into my arm and upward into my brain. And as if there were no words—no alphabets or even sounds—the vibrations reassembled in my mind as a silent image of the white moon against the black sky.

For although it is said that the moon is a stone orb floating in space—I know that's not true. The truth is that space is a curved black surface through which a hole has been pierced, allowing through it the resplendent whiteness of Heaven.

And that's what my hammer did—allowed a glowing circle of Heavenly whiteness to enter this world, while on the kitchen table, attempting to cry out, mother choked on the very oatmeal that was by then scorching her flesh.

4

The room that Jeremy kept in his mother's house—the room furthest away from her bedroom—was like a soft spot in the Earth's skull; a place where he could burrow in, hidden and protected.

The room hung heavy with a mustiness, as if a mass of spongy mushrooms flourished beneath the floorboards, causing them to bend and warp. And although Jeremy did all of his painting in there, it was hardly ideal for such an enterprise, for the windows, which were stained a sickening shade of brown from the foul moisture of the room, allowed in only specks of sunlight that dappled the walls like a disease of the skin. Luminous measles. Radiant impetigo.

Yet, the room was his constant companion—his protector—for only when absolutely necessary did he leave it; and then, only by the back door, never through the door leading to the rest of the house; and he kept both doors locked at all times, allowing no one admittance. His actual contact with his mother was minimal to the point of being non-existent. Yet, her presence managed to plague him day and night—usually in the form of convulsive bouts of rage in which she berated and belittled him. No walls, no matter how thick, were formidable enough to protect him from that.

Sometimes, though, she plagued him in other ways; ones that were more subtle and terrorizing. On those occasions, he would hear her in the garden out back; her footsteps echoing among the dead bushes and leprous gray lichens clinging to the moldering rock wall. He would hear her bare feet tamping down pebbles like smoldering coals; and her toenails scraping the earth like thick yellow talons; and her tail dragging behind her, leaving a trail in its wake like a sidewinder.

Standing in his room, frozen and silent, with only a thin wall between him and his mother, Jeremy would know without even seeing her that she was then pulling a pill bottle from her ragged robe...pulling it from beneath the flap of cloth covering her withered breasts from which viscous milk seeped and slowly leaked into the ground, poisoning the soil like dirty blood.

One blue pill...two blue pills...three...until his mother returned to her bedroom and succumbed to a dark and dreamless sleep.

It was only then, in those hours when she was unconscious, that Jeremy experienced some semblance of peace, and his painting flourished for it. Putting colors to canvas, bringing worlds to life—it was an act of love as far back as he could remember. And, too, it had a delicious tension to it—simultaneously opening the world to him *while also* protecting him from it.

On canvas, his fantasies came alive—often in hues so dark that, upon first glance, his paintings appeared to be abstractions with little tonal variation. Yet, upon closer examination, they might be revealed to depict the soundless depths of outer space; or the abdomen of a dead black beetle; or a decaying landscape and an ill-formed creature— legless, faceless, amorphous—skulking over it.

His paintings possessed the rare quality to both bewitch and repel the onlooker. That is, had there been any such onlookers to see them. For, Jeremy's reclusive nature severely limited the potential for his paintings to find an audience; and his mother, being the one person who might actually see them, would at best ridicule them as "pathetic abominations," and at worst ignore them entirely—just as she had ignored him all of his life.

She did everything she could to deny him his own identity—his own voice in the world—and relished doing so. For, although he was free to move about the house—free even to traverse the globe if he so pleased—he did not feel free; but instead felt as if his heart had been locked inside a metal box and his body locked inside a coffin that she kept beneath her bed. Most days, it was all Jeremy could do to hang onto even the tiniest sliver of who he truly was.

5

Its center is a white dwarf star; a densely packed frenzy of fragmented matter; and from that, dendrites splay out in a circular fashion—a blooming of black fissures spread across a silvery sky. There's a blotch of blood too, as if painted on by a child with a sponge, and a bit of fluttering skin clings to one of the fissures.

There had to have been an instant when her face, her reflection, and the fractured mirror almost coalesced, so closely did the three come together, but in the midst of the savagery there was no time to notice such subtleties. Which is a pity.

The countertop is littered with all manner of debris: toppled pill bottles, scattered pills, smashed bottles of vodka and wine, and powders and creams and balms all strewn about. And the floor is no better: shattered glass clinging to heaps of dirty clothes, sweat-stained bras, panties, towels, three Jack in the Box bags jammed full with Taco Bell wrappers, and a clump of bloody hair.

By comparison, the scene in the bathtub is one of relative serenity. That is, if you can ignore the shower curtain that has been ripped free from every hook but one. Mother is nude, which I regret, but circumstances dictated that. Yet, the water has a certain quality that diminishes the obscenity of it, making her appear unreal—almost like a mannequin—but one that has become, if not exactly bloated, at least softer around the edges. Gone from her face with the animating spirit are also any remnants of rage and narcissism. From her head, her hair gently sways like seaweed on the ocean floor, and from her nostrils, a trickle of blood dilutes into a winding trail of pink, which lends its hue to all of the water, so that the whole tableau is seen as if through rosé colored glasses.

I can still feel my hands around her throat; her windpipe collapsing against my pressure; her hand clawing the air in search of my face; while her other hand pulled down the shower curtain one hook at a time...pop, pop, pop. She was completely and utterly helpless against me. So weak, so impotent, so fragile. It was like crushing a blind baby bird. Silencing it before it had a chance to sing a single note of its appalling song.

6

Jeremy very rarely ventured outside of his room, because the world beyond his back door was not a pretty one. Simply catching a glimpse of it through his only window could induce anxiety and despair. The backyard was so derelict that even the living things in it seemed dead: bloodless weeds...black, liquescent mushrooms...gray moss...anemic vines. And the world beyond that—the blighted neighborhood that surrounded him—was no better. But sometimes Jeremy had no choice but to come face-to-face with it when he needed food or art supplies.

Such was the case one night just after he had completed a painting that he was especially pleased with. Standing before his creation, he pulled on his coat and squashed a toboggan down onto his head. But even after he had bundled up, he lingered a moment more, soaking in his artwork, as if it could somehow bolster him for his excursion into the cold and dreary world beyond his door.

The painting, like so many of his works, consisted mainly of dark hues—rich layers of blues, purples and blacks—but in the midst of all that darkness was a rare thing: a resplendent circle of heavenly whiteness that seemed to be, not a part of the darkness, but something that was *bursting through it*, as if from some blessed realm of light behind it. It was Jeremy's hope that he could carry that circle of whiteness within himself as he went out into the night.

As was always the case, he was careful to lock his back-door when he left. He then trudged through his backyard and made his way across the street, before cutting through the parking lot of the Floridian Motel, where vacant picnic tables sat on a narrow strip of dead grass outside the rooms. Up near the front office, yellow-orange flames in a fire pit were jittering against the darkness, and Jeremy saw that on the wall outside the office someone had used silver spray paint to write the words: **Slo Deth.**

It was bitter cold, but Jeremy could see silhouettes out in front of The Dutch and could hear loud laughter coming from them. As he drew closer to the bar's brightly burning neon lights, he noticed a black woman wearing a short tight skirt, who was sitting on a newspaper machine that had been turned on its side. Her legs were spread, her elbows were on her knees, and her face, hidden behind a mass of hair, was in her hands. She was perfectly still, maybe unconscious. On the sidewalk beneath her was a small pool of pink vomit. To her side, three skinny white girls were hanging on each other, stumbling and laughing loudly. As Jeremy passed them, he heard one of them go, "I'm just not attracted to the mentally disabled...is that such a crime?"

Their resulting laughter rang in his ears long after he had passed them. He had no doubt that the woman's comment had been directed at him.

Turning the corner, Jeremy passed by the out-of-business pager store, the out-of-business church, the out-of-business wig shop where wigs were still displayed behind darkened windows. Then he made his way down an alley, until he came to Ogie's Carry-Out, where he bought most of his food. As he made his way across the parking lot, he cringed at the sight of a white boy and two black girls standing near the door. The only things as unpredictable as women were little girls.

Thankfully, they didn't seem to notice him. When he got near the door, he saw that there was a small plastic aquarium on the ground near the boy's feet, and that they were all distracted by a thick black snake that he was holding in his hands and showing to them. Slowly, the girls inched closer to him, until the boy jabbed the reptile at them, and the girls grabbed each other and scurried backwards and squealed and doubled-over with laughter.

Jeremy's nerves prickled with every sound they made. Once inside the store, he quickly made his way up and down the aisles, gathering up some of his staples: sardines, crackers, Coke. He kept his head down and his eyes averted, hoping to avoid any human contact; especially that of the skinny black woman running the register, who always tried to make conversation with him no matter what he did to stave it off.

But, unfortunately, that night was no different than others, because as soon as Jeremy laid his items on the counter, the woman went, "Don't you never get tired of eatin them little fishes?"

"Um...what?" Jeremy mumbled.

"Them sardines," she went, as she started scanning his items. "Don't you never get tired of em? I couldn't live on nothin but little fishes. I like me a burger too much!"

"Well, there's crackers..."

"Okay, okay, I guess...but still. I mean, you ain't never gonna grow up to be big and strong if you don't ever eat no real meat!"

A big loud laugh burst from the woman's mouth as she handed Jeremy his bag; and as he accepted it, he turned away, avoiding eye contact, and ducked his head down low as he hurried out of the store.

Thankfully, the kids were no longer in the parking lot, and he was fortunate, too, in that his entire walk back home was without incident. But, truthfully, it would have taken something astonishing for him to have noticed it, because he was so caught up in trying to figure out why that woman back at the store had to be so malicious; why she insisted on belittling him every single time he went in there.

I'm a paying customer, not just some bum off the street! How can you have the nerve to judge me? I'm an artist! And what're you? Nothing! A pathetic woman at a pathetic job. Yet, you take it out on me. You want to pull me down to your level, or even lower, so that you can stand on top of me. But why? Is it because I'm a man? Is that it? Well, this man can only be pushed around so much before he does something about it, and you have no idea what I'm capable of. I could do whatever I wanted to you, and there'd be nothing you could do about it. Then you'd find out who's small! Then you'd find out who's weak!

For his entire walk home, such thoughts boiled inside him, but as soon as his house was within sight, those thoughts turned off like a faucet and were instantly replaced by a white hot panic at what he saw. A sickly brown rectangle of light was being cast out onto the walkway from his back door, which was wide open for all the world to see. The bag of groceries tumbled from his hands, and Jeremy ran toward the house. It was a short run and he covered the ground quickly, but when he crossed the threshold, his breaths were already coming fast and heavy, and the thump of his heartbeat thundered in his ears. He came to a sudden halt in the middle of the room, and his eyes rapidly scanned it, trying to see every inch of it all at once. It was obvious that the intruder was no longer there, but Jeremy had no doubt that someone had been there a short time before he arrived. He could feel it in the marrow of his bones.

Jeremy took a deep breath, trying to calm his frazzled nerves as he started back toward the door in order to close it, but before he reached it, something out of the corner of his eye caused his heart, which had been jumping around in his chest, to suddenly go as cold and still as a stone. He saw that his painting—the one he had completed just before leaving for the store—had been defaced. The heavenly circle of whiteness had been painted over; covered in a hideously thick smear of black; and at the sight of it, any remnant of the circle that he still carried within himself was extinguished.

Stumbling backwards, Jeremy's legs found his bed just in time to save him from collapsing onto the floor. Hot tears welled up in his eyes and streamed down his cheeks, and his body quaked inside and out.

This was a violation that he could not allow to go unpunished.

7

Strangulation: the most personal form of death.
It must be performed with the bare hands, not with a rope

or a belt or other such implement. And one must be able to look deep into her eyes as one performs it, so that one can witness the transformation from panic to resignation to a final fading to gray.

Silently, I open my bedroom door. It has been so long since I last used this entryway into the rest of the house that even the knob feels peculiar in my hand; and as I step into the hallway, the shadows upon the walls seem both familiar and utterly foreign; and the stagnant, musty smell of the house, which clings to my skin as I slowly wade through it, is like a distant, faded memory, dating as far back, perhaps, as my initial sojourn inside her stifling womb.

As I pass from the hallway to the living room, each adornment I lay my eyes upon seems as if from a dream—but a recurring one—so that there is both a familiarity and a mystery to everything. The framed pictures upon the walls must be of relatives— aunts, uncles, grandparents, and great-grandparents—but how is it possible that I have gone so long without thinking of any of them? So long, in fact, that they now appear almost like strangers to my eyes. And this curious statuette on the end table; I recognize it; it is some type of serpent, poised to strike; but it seems years since I last laid eyes upon it. Yet, here it remains, suspended forever in its threatening posture. Even the bottle of pills next to it has a familiarity to it. Although, it could not have always occupied that same spot, could it? But perhaps it did. Perhaps it was always there; always at the ready for when her brain was in need of numbing.

The sputtering snores I hear are also known to me, but seem to return to me from across a great distance. They are an obscene thing—warm and viscous—and are accompanied by a miserable, erratic whistling from her nose. As I gaze down upon her lying *supine on the couch, I note that her mouth hangs wide open, as if she has grown slack-jawed and feebleminded, but I know nothing can be further from the truth; for, although her litany of faults is long, a lack of intelligence is not one of them.*

She is a hideous and pathetic sight to behold. Her mauve lipstick is wildly askew, giving her lips a contorted appearance, and her hair, so matted and patchy, gives the impression of being a cheap wig that has been squashed down upon her head. But most repugnant of all is that she sleeps with one eye open. Rheumy and cadaverous, it yet remains all-seeing and all-knowing. Its reach is unlimited; it sees through walls; it passes judgment from afar. It is an evil eye, from which there is no known form of protection. It holds you in its gaze, paralyzes you, and then peels away your layers—your skin, your muscle, your bones—until you are nothing. Nothing at all. But even as nothing, you remain trapped in its harsh glare, completely at its mercy.

But that is all about to come to an end...

My bare hands are at the ready, hovering before me like two claws, as I bend at the waist, holding my breath tightly in my chest so as to not give off even the slightest of sounds. A tremble in my hands travels up my arms and settles, fluttering, in my heart, as I move in so closely that I begin to smell the decay emanating from her gaping mouth. Above her larynx, my thumbs linger, and my fingers curve in anticipation of constricting her neck. With a steady hiss, I permit my breath to slowly seep from between my slightly parted lips. And perhaps that is what wakes her...

Perhaps that is why both of her eyes have snapped open and are staring wildly at me, trying to comprehend what is happening, and what will be happening, and what it could all mean.

Intently, I stare back into those very eyes and begin to squeeze with all my might. The transformation has begun...from panic to resignation to a final fading to gray.

8

His hands rested on his thighs. The trembling he saw in them was now from rage, not fear—a rage that would not abate on its own, but would have to culminate before it could be calmed. Jeremy's hands slid from his thighs and fell to his sides as he stood up from his bed. Beneath him, his legs were both shaky and strong from the adrenaline flooding his body. Beyond his bedroom door, he knew his mother must be screeching and cackling—belittling him with her every utterance—but the surge of blood in his ears drowned her out.

There was a strong temptation—almost a magnetic pull—to look at the mutilated painting; to witness once again the stain upon his Heavenly circle of whiteness; but he resisted, focusing instead on the punishment that must ensue. He began to walk toward his bedroom door. With each step, he tried to calm his ragged breaths by inhaling deeply through his nostrils and exhaling slowly from his mouth, so that by the time he grasped the doorknob, he had reduced the trembling in his hands to a faint vibration. Yet, he still paused before turning the knob, as a shudder of uncertainty shook inside him, as he wondered if he was truly capable of committing the act that he knew must come. For a moment, he even considered turning back; considered falling into his bed and curling up, tight as a nut, with his hands desperately clamped over his ears, trying to drown out the taunts to come. But deep down, he knew there was no turning back. If he did, the taunts would never end...and the small amount of peace he had would be gone forever...and his paintings—his only voice in the world—would always be in danger of being defaced, silencing him forever.

Tears began to well up, but Jeremy fought them back as he turned the doorknob, using one of the very same hands that would soon be upon his mother's throat. Soundlessly, the door swung open, and he took a step into the hallway, but then hesitated. Something didn't feel right. In fact, *everything felt wrong*. There seemed to be too much light, and it was so bright that his eyes ached at the sight and cowered into a squint. It was too quiet—moments before, his mother was screeching and cackling; now he heard nothing; a silence so intense it made the flesh on his arms stand up.

Jeremy remained frozen in his tracks for several seconds as he tried to make sense of it, but there was no sense to be made. As his eyes adjusted to the light, he saw neither a hallway nor the rooms beyond, but instead a beautiful, confusing scene. By leaving his room, he had not entered the rest of the house, but had *emerged from it*, and suddenly found himself standing beneath a brilliant blue sky and upon an abundantly green earth. Before him, a single majestic tree with branches stretching out in every direction—like the mighty arms of a many-limbed god—beckoned him into its bosom.

If he could only break free from his stasis—if he could move forward even a single step—he sensed something would happen, something would change, but he remained frozen, mesmerized but fearful

Could this be it? Could this be the true Heavenly circle of whiteness? Not a mere blob of white paint smeared onto a canvas, but a

true opening...a true ingress to the light.

His body trembled. His hands—the hands of a potential strangler, a potential matricide—quaked uncontrollably.

But what will mother say if I stir even an inch further? What will she do to punish such an act of brazen independence?

To move backward—to return to the womb of his room—would have been easy. He merely had to do it; he just had to take a step backward, which he knew his body and mind would allow. To move forward, he sensed, was also possible, even though it *felt* impossible. It wouldn't take much—he knew that—and yet somehow it would take everything.

I only need to make the smallest of movements. The infinitesimal wiggle of a fingertip...the tiniest twitch of a toe...

There he remained, frozen.

For how long, no can say.

Flight

Have you heard of the young woman who was afraid of flying?

She went through therapy and made several, ultimately aborted attempts to fly on a plane. Eventually, however, she broke through and went on a flight. Once in the air, she was ecstatic—the flight was not frightening; it was exhilarating!

That was, until she was invited by a stewardess to visit the cockpit, where she found, to her horror, that the plane was being flown by kangaroos.

Acknowledgements

As I prepared these stories for publication, I received invaluable advice from Sondra Snodgrass, Rob Jackson and Michele Reinhart. Sondra did a wonderful job of suggesting "big picture" changes; Rob did a wonderful job of suggesting "little picture" changes; and Michele was kind enough to tell me when something was just plain bad, which may be the most valuable type of advice any writer can receive. I thank you all for your kindness, time and effort.

I also want to thank Dave Megenhardt for helping to edit and layout the book, as well as giving me the opportunity to publish it. You're not only a damn good writer, but you're a damn good guy too.

Finally, I want to thank Joe Snodgrass for the fantastic design they came up with for the cover. It captures the feel of the stories, and more importantly, looks like something I'd instantly be drawn to as a reader. Check out Joe's other artwork at the Instagram account "loveisformortals".

www.ingramcontent.com/pod-product-compliance
Lightning Source LLC
Chambersburg PA
CBHW030131260626
47156CB00008B/2888